WINTER WOLVES

A ROAMER WESTERN

WINTER WOLVES

MATTHEW P. MAYO

FIVE STAR
A part of Gale, a Cengage Company

GALE
A Cengage Company

LIBRARY OF CONGRESS CATALOGING-IN-PUBLICATION DATA

Names: Mayo, Matthew P., author.
Title: Winter wolves / Matthew P Mayo.
Description: First edition. | Waterville : Five Star, 2021. | Series: A Roamer Western
Identifiers: LCCN 2021022279 | ISBN 9781432887322 (hardcover)
Subjects: GSAFD: Western stories.
Classification: LCC PS3613.A963 W56 2021 | DDC 813/.6—dc23
LC record available at https://lccn.loc.gov/2021022279

First Edition. First Printing: November 2021
Find us on Facebook—https://www.facebook.com/FiveStarCengage
Visit our website—http://www.gale.cengage.com/fivestar
Contact Five Star Publishing at FiveStar@cengage.com

Printed in Mexico
Print Number: 01   Print Year: 2022

To Mom and Dad.
And to the woods, the waters, the wild places . . .
my apologies, and my thanks.

I went to the woods because I wished to live deliberately . . . and not, when I came to die, discover that I had not lived. . . .

—*Walden*, Henry David Thoreau

PROLOGUE

The last time I faced down a pack of winter-starved timber wolves was . . . never. So waking up and hearing panting and snuffling and low snarls circling not twenty feet from my paltry campfire was a tip-off that all was not well in my little hunk of wilderness.

I blinked and tried to figure out who I was, where I was, and why I was there. The moon, somewhere between a thin and a thick sliver, offered enough blue glow on this cloudless night that I saw a dark shape closing in on me. That's when the first wolf lunged.

But I should back up a step and tell you how I got into that situation in the first place . . .

CHAPTER ONE

It was a fine, finger-snap morning in early December when I set down my coffee cup and stifled a belch. I may be a whole lot of things—big, homely, a frightener of children and timid folks—but I am not a savage. I will say, even if I had belched loud and long, that meal was worthy of risking public embarrassment.

I'd indulged in a mounded platter of roasted beef so tender it tasted as if it had stewed in its juices for days. Right beside that on the pewter platter sat a pile of boiled potatoes, each the size of a baby's head, well salted and peppered, and dolloped with a thumb-size knob of rich butter the deep yellow of the eye of a daisy flower. Ladled over that, steamed thick, near-black, chunky gravy, enough so the spuds and meat got good and saturated.

At the same time, I sipped a cup of hot coffee splashed with fresh cream—an indulgence I never seem to find on the trail, try as I might (I still haven't worked up the nerve to milk a sow grizz). I followed that wondrous feed with a wedge—okay, two wedges—of pie.

The first was a mixed-berry delight with huckleberries, black raspberries, and strawberries. The matron who ran the place said she'd dried them using a method an old African woman taught her. I commended them both. The juice ran dark and sweet all over the little stoneware plate. It did not escape me, though—I sopped it up with the last lardy, flaky crumbs of the crust.

The second wedge of pie was a chocolate confection, made

to be eaten chilled. It had gelled somehow, so that it wobbled when I prodded it with my fork. I'd not had anything like that out here on the frontier, and it was as rich as it looked, and beyond delicious. Or, as my friend Maple Jack would say, it tasted like . . . more.

And that's what led me to nearly belch in public.

I tell you what—no lie—as good as that meal was, and as I say, it was fine, it did not quite measure up to most any campfire meal conjured—moans and gripes and curses and sneers and all—by my good friend and mentor, the aforementioned Maple Jack. He's a knob-gutted, buckskin wearing, mountain goat of an old man who, if he ever heard I referred to him as such, would savage me with that chipped, well-oiled, stud-handled tomahawk he wears tucked in his waist sash as if it were part of him. Come to think on it, I've rarely seen him without it.

Speaking of Maple Jack, I intended to take him up on his years-long offer of visiting him and his "winter woman" up by Salish Lake in Montana Territory. He offers this each autumn before he heads up there himself. This year, I believed I'd do it. I've said so in the past, and never made it beyond view of the distant peaks. First things first, though. I had supplies to purchase. Before my excellent meal, I'd left my list of requirements off at the local mercantile.

I'd ridden into Two-Penny the evening before, bundled in my wool red-and-black check mackinaw, its woolly sheep-hide collar turned up to save my face and ears from the nippy night air. I'd been to the little burg before, maybe three years since. I recalled it as one of the few places where the local lawdog hadn't made an effort to turn me around and send me on my way.

You see, I'm not what you'd call handsome. In fact, my name is Scorfano, which in Italian means "Ugly One." It was a name given me by my mother and father. The mater was shocked that something so hideous could have emerged "squallerin'," as Jack says, from her loins. Especially since she was the recipient of nothing but good fortune in her lifetime, being born into a life of relative wealth and comfort as the daughter of a Virginia plantation owner.

She married a dashing Italian, a philanderer as it turns out, of low character and little money. He did have a spit-shined title of some sort, which in her eyes made him worthy of her fluttering affections.

By the time my younger brother came along, they had already fobbed me off on Mimsy, the cook, who raised me on the old home place. On the eve of my fourteenth birthday, I overheard her conversing in whispers with a young housemaid. They were both in their cups and indulging in gossip-mongering. It loosed Mimsy's razor tongue and she revealed my life story to the girl.

Stunned and speechless in the shadows, that very night I stole my father's favorite racehorse and made my way West. I was large for my age, and as long as I kept my mouth closed, I passed myself off as a green, yet full-grown, man.

My fists made up for what mental acuity I lacked, particularly when confronted with life's crueler denizens and situations, which I found in abundance on the trail. To be fair, these rogues and moments were, if not balanced with, at least smoothed by occasional kindnesses from strangers. These folks were often those who, like me, found themselves traveling the shadowed edges of society because of false assumptions made by "good citizens."

I speak of black families seeking peace and safety away from the foolish cruelty of bigotry and unwarranted hatred. I speak of Indians who wished to live as their forebears, the very people who roamed this vast land before any whites from Europe rowed ashore. And I speak of so many more, the shunned of the road.

Among them I felt, for the first time, somewhat welcome. Yet even among them, as large and as homely as I am, I felt their fear and saw their wary glances, saw them hug their children close. It began to occur to me, over the long, lean weeks, then months, then years on my own, that I would forever be alone in the world.

And yet I now say, with gratitude, that has not proven to be the case. For I have Tiny Boy, my Percheron stallion, as stalwart a chum as a man could hope to find. I suspect there's a dog out there somewhere in my future travels who may also qualify for such a role in my life. Or perhaps I in his.

And I have Maple Jack, who saved my sorry hide in the midst of a blizzard, back when I was, as he says, "a shivering whelp." He became the only true human friend I have ever had. And with him, that is all the friend I need. Not to say he isn't a crotchety old thing, for he is that, and more. And I wouldn't change him if I could, not only because I'd draw back a bloody stump should I try. No, he's steadfast and true and that's all a man can ask of a pal in this life.

CHAPTER TWO

The morning after I arrived in Two-Penny, I entered the rather grandly named Houghton's Emporium of Necessities. A brass bell clanged above my head and the proprietor looked me up, down, and up again, over the top of his half-moon spectacles. Then he nodded and smiled.

Could be he had somehow determined I was not set on robbing him or killing him. It may have been that my homely face was half hidden by my coat's collar. Or perhaps he was kind. I chose to believe the latter. I tugged off a glove with my teeth and reached in my coat for my list. He didn't flinch. An auspicious start, I thought.

I handed him my list and he looked it over, nodding and making a whistling sound through his nostrils as he breathed.

"I thought I'd visit the diner for a meal. I have a couple of other stops to make." I let that hang in the air between us a moment.

When he realized I wasn't going to follow that with a question, he looked up and nodded. "Right, sir," he said, eyeing the list and surprising me with a Scots accent, the burrs somewhat sanded off the edges, no doubt by time spent in the New World. "I can have this ready for you by . . . midday?" He looked up.

"That would be fine. Thank you." I turned to face the well-lit room. Not a man afraid to brighten the corners.

The potbelly stove in the center of the room was as yet unoccupied by the usual contingent of tale-tellers and cracker eaters.

15

They'd show soon, they always do, no matter the town, no matter the season. I wanted to be gone before they dribbled in to stare at me, before they commenced to gnaw the same bones they did every day.

The interiors of general mercantile shops have always fascinated me. Not because they are filled with things I wish to possess, for I have all, well, most, of what I require. They intrigue me because they are filled with a bonanza of color outdone only by autumn's leafy splendors when nature closes up shop and draws inward. And because the products themselves represent places far from where I happen to be, namely roaming the West in search of . . . what, Roamer? What is it you are seeking?

Houghton's Emporium of Necessities was no letdown. I spied tins and boxes with fancy labels and fancier curlicue script denoting the contents within, be they buttons from France or lavender-scented shaving soaps. I saw blue denim shirts and rough-cloth work trousers the color of pine bark, black boots gleaming with polish, and tight-woven baskets suspended from ceiling joists. All of it was a sight to behold, and none of it tempted me. Save for one thought, unlikely as it was. Still, can it ever hurt to wonder?

Behind me, the merchant cleared his throat. "Would there be anything I might help you with?"

I almost said no, then reminded myself that it is at such moments when life can surprise us. "Well . . ." I turned to face him. "You wouldn't happen to have any books for sale, would you?"

"Books?" he repeated, saying the word softly as though speaking it *sotto voce* from the lip of a stage to an intimate, rapt crowd.

I was ready to say it was all right, I understood it was an unusual request, particularly in a small town, and such and such and on and on before blushing and making for the door. That was my usual manner of handling such a situation. For despite my best efforts to the contrary, it had happened before. Where books are concerned, I cannot help myself. But this fellow surprised me.

"Of course, of course!" He smiled as he lifted the hinged section of countertop and ducked out from behind. "Follow me, sir."

And so I did. He seemed a man true to his word. In a back corner, beyond the shelves of new boots and a display of coils of rope, a shelf held four volumes, none overly similar to the others in size, shape, or, as I soon saw, in content. Alexandre Dumas's *The Count of Monte Cristo;* James Fenimore Cooper's *The Pathfinder,* one of his five Leatherstocking Tales novels; and Charles Dickens's *David Copperfield.* I noted in silence and with an inward sigh that I'd already become acquainted with those three. Then I read the spine of the fourth and last, a green board copy of *Leaves of Grass* by Walt Whitman. I pointed to the book. "May I?"

He nodded with enthusiasm.

I slid the book out and admired its heft in my hand. I had read several of Whitman's poems in various newspapers over the years and liked them. This collection held promise. Though it had been read and well-thumbed, the crispness of the printing on the opening pages made me smile, bold black letters on a creamy colored paper, thick with what looked like mouse-nibbled edges where the paper was hand-torn and not sliced.

I rarely lust after something, except for a good meal and a bracing hot cup of coffee. Perhaps to a lesser degree a folding knife. I have two and do not tire of gazing at new ones in shop display cases.

Put a book in front of me and my normally steady heartbeat *thump-thumps* an extra time or two. That green book elicited three thumps. I wanted it.

"Ah, how much are you asking?"

The man rubbed his chin, knowing he had me over a barrel. He'd seen it on my face, no doubt. Perhaps, too, it surprised him as it has others in the past that a man of a size and with a countenance such as mine might be interested in the written word. Several people have gone as far as to baldly ask if I could read. Hmm, I say.

"Considering you are obviously a reading man, I could let that book be yours for . . ."

I waited, holding the book closed in both my big hands, as if an offering to be laid on an altar. I am not impoverished, but I do not like to be taken advantage of, and as much as I wanted the book, the next thing he said would determine if I was about to add a new tome to my meager yet choice traveling library, or if it would stay on his shop shelf, waiting for the next reader to come along. I held my breath.

"One dollar."

I let out my breath quietly. It was not a bargain price, but given the hours of pure enjoyment I would gain from the book, it was a price I could agree to. "Sold," I said, smiling. I handed it to him, with reluctance. "Would you mind holding it until I pick up my order? It would prove too great a distraction to me and I want to enjoy every word."

He nodded, still smiling. "As a fellow bibliophile, I understand. Might I say I doubt it will let you down." He leaned close and touched a side of his nose as if he were sharing a deep secret, though to my knowledge we were alone in the store. "It has been one of my favorites and I thought twice about bringing it out into the shop."

"Well, I'm pleased you did, sir," I said, hoping he wouldn't tell me any more about the book. In a life such as mine, perhaps in everyone's lives, surprise is all. Like the man of ordinary magic I had begun to suspect he was, he read my mind and only nodded and led the way back to the front of the store.

There were other things I would need to peruse in that shop. I would save them for later, when I picked up my order before I departed from Two-Penny.

I bid him good day and, chin up and smiling, rare for me in a town as I prefer to keep my maw down and my hat brim tugged low, I clomped down the boardwalk. I passed townsfolk who behave as they always do when they see me—they averted their eyes. The bravest offered nervous smiles that flitted from their faces as soon as I passed. My mood only dampened slightly when I walked by the constable's office. I had no desire to endure yet another unwarranted harassment.

Besides, I had errands to get up to, not a task I pursue with any great frequency. I was hungry, I needed a few lengths of scrap leather, and I had fleeting thoughts of seeking out a newspaper. The town had grown since I last visited, and that many residents would surely demand news that hadn't been passed from lip to ear to lip to ear for weeks or months, teasing apart and re-forming in unintended ways until the morsel had become out-proportioned to its initial intent and meaning, pinched and struggling under the weight of fallacy.

Luck was with me. The town of Two-Penny did indeed sport a new-looking sign swinging three doors down from a dusty-fronted saloon that looked as though it would not open for many hours yet. The sign read *Two-Penny Gazette and Informer, Campion Fisk, Editor and Proprietor.*

Once again, the burgeoning town failed to disappoint me. I thumbed the latch, a fancy carved brass affair, and pushed open the door of the shop. Once more I thrust out a quick breath of resignation. Such visits in the past had not ended well. Another bell overhead, this time more of a tinkling sound, announced my presence.

There was only one man in the print shop. As I assessed him and waited for him to greet me, I breathed deep of the place's singular smells. There was a sharp, chemical-laden tang to the air that I believe emanates from the ink. More pleasant was the smell of light oil and metal working together to prevent machinery from squawking and grinding itself apart. I also smelled the usual guttering, smoky lamp-stink pervading the room's shaded interior.

As my eyes grew accustomed, I noted trays stacked in a rack, layered such that each successive tray, from the floor to about man-height, sat canted back several inches. I had not seen this manner of type rack and found it of interest.

"Okay, then," said the man I'd seen. He was a thin, youngish fellow with little hair on his pate except a curly black fringe about his head. It winged out over his ears and trailed down to long, thick, and fuzzy muttonchop sideburns that nearly met at the point of his long chin. This look appeared to be a cultivation of which he was proud. He shouldn't have been. It gave his already long, bony face a vulpine look. He canted his head to one side and eyed me through small, round, brass-rim spectacles, further accentuating his harried-bird features. His smock, a once-white affair, was stained with great dark smudges of black ink, as were his fingers, his nose tip, and cheeks. "How may I be of service to you?"

I nodded and smiled. "I am in the market for news, new or old, anything readable, really. I have been long in the bush and I wish to reacquaint myself with the doings of humanity."

He cracked a smile and wagged a long fingertip at me in a scolding manner. "You may well regret that, once you find out what the world has been up to in your absence." He turned and in two long strides carried himself to the back of the room. He rummaged atop a desk that was piled far too high and deep with paper, paper, and more paper, none in tidy stacks. How did he ever get any work done?

Where did the man write his news? What brought him to this

place, I wondered as I waited. And so, feeling bold, I asked him.

"Oh, I am originally . . ." He grunted and shoved papers aside. "From a little place back East called Providence."

"Hardly little," I said.

He looked over his shoulder at me. "You know of it, then?"

I nodded. "The seat of power in a small state big on ambition."

"Indeed. And even bigger on boldness." He returned to me with a stack perhaps an inch thick of single-sheet newspapers, printed on both sides. And bearing as a banner atop each, the name I'd seen on the sign out front: *The Two-Penny Gazette and Informer.*

"This should do me fine," I said, accepting them.

"Now, don't blame me if you read these and find yourself thinking dark thoughts." He smiled and wagged that scolding finger once more. "It's none of my doing that the world of men is an oddity best left unexamined. Or at least that's how the jaded journalist in me feels much of the time these days."

"I'll do my best to remain jovial."

"Excellent."

"What do I owe you?"

He blew out a breath between his thin lips, then nibbled the bottom one. "Oh, ah, I'm no good with such things. Part of the reason I left Providence behind. Too much exciting news and far too much attention from creditors. Then again, you may be one and I'd not know it, eh?"

"Debt collection is not one of the things in this life I aspire to, I promise you that."

"Tell you what, you tell me your tale, a big fellow like you spending much time amongst nature and little else, at least that's my guess, and we'll call it even."

I admired his instinct for scaring up a story, yet I've no desire to have my life poked, probed, and prodded by a newspaperman. Ever. "I'd as soon give you cold, hard cash and call it even."

He sighed. "Alas, no news is . . . no news." He shrugged. "How about a nickel?"

"For the lot?" I said, my raised eyebrows matching the surprise in my voice.

"Too much?"

I shook my head. "Do yourself a favor, Mr. Fisk, and marry a woman who keeps books and . . ." My eyes roved over his shoulder to the desk in the back. "Doesn't mind organizing stacks of paper."

I pushed a dollar into his hand and gave him a two-finger salute off my eyebrow. "Thanks for the news." I opened the door and as the bell ceased tinkling above my head, I said, "I think."

He nodded and turned back to his task of setting type, a smile on his face and concentration knitting his brow once more.

I had romanticized the occupation of a newsman and printer as a high calling filled with intriguing moments and deep rumination. I saw now that while it could well be those things, it was likely often a lonely life for little reward. I hoped for Mr. Fisk's sake that my assessment was far from that mark.

On leaving the printer's office I gazed up and down the street, reclaiming my bearings, and said, "Mm-hmm," as I spied the diner. Would it be possible that each establishment I visited in Two-Penny treated me as an anyone and a no one, two guises I am rarely allowed to don? I'd soon find out.

It was late enough in the morning that I might not be saddled with the usual fare of undercooked eggs and too-salty ham steak, and potatoes fried in grease with a bowl of baked beans on the side. I've nothing against any of these foods, prepared well, but my morning meals are usually scant, by choice. I find that other than a pot full of strong coffee and several cups of water, should I be encamped by a stream, which I always try to do, I prefer the clearheaded feeling that lack of morning food gives me.

I ride and walk the trails, and forge my own paths, sometimes much to Tiny Boy's perturbation, with little more than a general direction in mind. Thus unencumbered by a packed gut and a sluggish gait, I am able to ponder much of whatever surrounds me, which more often than not I find of great interest.

If one has a clear head and is fortunate enough to travel on a clear day in pleasant temperatures—not blustery or frigid or pelting rain or sizzling in bald sunshine—the smallest of details make themselves clear. There are all manner of tiny birds that make little more than a murmuring sound as they go about their business of pecking tree bark for bugs I've yet to be able to spot. There are bushy-tail squirrels, slate in color, with the darkest eyes of any creature I've seen. I am certain, however, that this characteristic, given their tiny fits of rage, does not reveal the content of their souls. Anything that unwittingly amusing is a fine beast, in my opinion.

There is so much to see and feel and do, I think to myself frequently, and so little time between now and whatever end may be out there for me.

Jack says I'm a ninny for what he calls "wasting my thinker" on such observations. I know he does much the same, given the details of his days' observations he has shared with me over campfires and a glug or three of his own brand of gullet-scorching liquor.

As I've already related the memorable repast I experienced at what was named, appropriately enough, the Two-Penny Diner, I won't repeat it, save to say that I wished I was hungry all over again simply to experience it once more before I took my leave of that fine little town.

Too soon, the last plate was all but licked clean and my bill was paid. The waitress even smiled when she took my money. Then I stepped back outside onto the nippy, bustling street.

CHAPTER THREE

I first visited the livery, where Tiny Boy was rested and waiting. I could tell his patience for such plush accommodation had worn through hours before. That's another trait I share with Tiny Boy. Itchy-feet is what Jack calls the restlessness people and horses get when they want to be good and gone from a place.

It's something I have experienced many times, and expect to many more. The best description I can offer is to say that *here* isn't *there* and *there* isn't *here*.

It's a peculiar feeling to never be quite satisfied with one's lot in life. I have grown accustomed to it, enough that most of the time I don't mind. It can wear on a body, though.

At such times I'll become morose and ponder past mistakes, wonder if I should have lingered longer here or there, settled in any one of a number of perfect little lonely valleys I've passed through, built a cabin beside a stream and planted a garden. Then I get to thinking about all the vistas I've not yet seen, all the smells unsniffed by me, all the weathers . . . And so, there is no end to it.

My intention was to load my panniers onto Tiny Boy's willing back. Well, *willing* may be wishful thinking. Without my weight on him, he's able to ferry a load with little bother, so I walk beside him, and lead whenever it's necessary. This arrangement suits us both, as neither of us has anywhere in particular to get to much of the time. Often, I am stopped by fellow travelers who inquire if my big horse is lame. *No,* I say. *I felt like walking a while.*

That mild response is far less apt to make them scratch their heads in wonder at why a man of my size should choose to lead a perfectly rideable beast. Truth is, I'm not a flower of a man and I feel guilty climbing aboard the big brute. I can't help wondering how I would feel were someone to do the same to me. Doesn't mean I don't ride him, though. And in truth, he seems not to mind in the least, perhaps he even enjoys it. That might be stretching the truth to suit my whims, however.

At some point, Tiny Boy will break my heart, I know. He'll succumb to age or an affliction or accident, same as any beast, man or otherwise. I also know, after some time, another horse will somehow cross my trail and we'll take up together.

It happened with Jake, a horse I had before Tiny. We were friends and trail mates for a number of years when a poorly aimed bullet intended for me lodged deep in his broad chest. It was a mortal wound and he would have bled to death inside had I not brought him to his end with my Smith & Wesson Schofield. The memory still guts me. His eye looking at me, his ragged breath huffing, blood snotting out his nostrils. I avenged him shortly thereafter and will dwell no more on it here.

On the whole, I find what humans like to call "animals," as if we are different from them, are a load easier to get along with than most any people I've ever met. It's not that I treat them special or make a fuss over them. I don't believe they want to be treated any differently than I wish to be. For the most part they tend to their own needs, as I do mine.

I find it amusing that nonhuman critters are attracted to me. If I didn't, I might be bothered that so-called savage creatures find my companionship more desirable than that of their kind. I sometimes wish women felt the same way. For that matter, anybody else. Thankfully, dogs and squirrels and horses and rabbits and birds and deer don't judge a person based on his looks. If they did, I would be well and truly alone more often than I am.

On that day, with our bellies full, not long past noon, I led Tiny Boy away from the loading dock behind Houghton's Emporium and on out of Two-Penny. The panniers, oversize canvas bags draped and secured behind the cantle, shifted lightly with their solid load, and once more we took to the open trail.

This time I had a destination in mind. I was headed to Maple Jack's place in the mountains north of here. He lives in the Sawtooths, in a cabin snugged like moss on a rock in a grove of quaking aspen. It's grizzly country, then again much of that region is. Jack likes it fine and, other than two-legged raiders, he's not come to much long-standing harm holed up in the mountains. It suits him, and it's always a fine respite for me, too. We catch up on news and chew the fat, as he says, over copious shares from his ever-present jug.

He will not be there, though, when I arrive in a week or so. He will instead be far north, up at Salish Lake, with Winter Woman. I don't even know if he knows her name, that's all he's ever called her, and he's been spending the coldest months with her for years now.

I've not met her, though Jack has invited me to spend time with them at her place to the north. She lives alone, and I've been assured there's a spare bunk she uses for midwifery. If it's not occupied by a pained, laboring mother-to-be when I arrive, I have been invited to pass the time there, with the understanding that if there's a bairn in the offing, I am to find a nearby tree to camp beneath. I believe I'll take the tree anyway.

Despite Jack's fondness for her and for the place in which she lives, I've not taken him up on this offer before now since I don't care for the awkwardness that such a visit will bring. The only reason I have changed my mind this year is because I have an ulterior motivation.

I intend to leave Tiny Boy with Jack, who'll care for him, alongside Ol' Mossback, Jack's mule, in the woman's stable. He has told me she has a donkey she uses to carry her doctoring supplies. She's a witchy woman. At least that's what Jack calls her. He says she's part of all tribes and a full member of none, part Salish, part Métis, part medicine woman, shaman, and healer, "and all wildcat." He winks when he says that part.

I can't fail to smile when I think of my old friend. He's old enough, I suspect, to be my father, and in every way that counts, he has filled that role to me. Yet he still cavorts like a young buck in springtime. I'd like to think I could be like him one day, though in truth, I know this will not come to pass. We are different people, Jack and I. That's part of what makes us friends, I think.

I plan on staying with them for a night or two, then I'll venture deeper into the mountains on snowshoe. Back in late August when I last spent time with Maple Jack, and when I mentioned my vague plans to him, he looked at me as if I'd slapped a baby in his presence.

"I knew all that reading of books and thinking all alone out there in the wild was making your brains soft, now I have proof! Snowshoe into the mountains in winter?" He made a sound from deep in his throat as if he were gagging on a nub of beef and shook his head.

Later, though, he asked me questions and warmed to the idea in that backdoor way only Jack has. By the time I left a couple of days after, he was claiming credit for planting the notion in my head, and lamenting that he couldn't go with me, to show me how to survive alone in the mountains in winter.

I smiled and said he was welcome to tag along. He puffed up, looked at his moccasins, and said he'd have to see how Winter

Woman felt about all this foolishness. Likely couldn't leave her alone for that long. I didn't point out that he'd told me several times with pride that the woman lived alone most of the year and had done so for longer than I'd been alive.

And so I walked along on that crisp day toward Jack's empty cabin. My plan was to drop off his supplies and pick up the snowshoes I made for myself at his place in the summer. I intended to spend a day or so there, repacking my gear and refreshing my reading stock—I have a shelf of books in his cabin. Given that various pages are dog-eared, I suspect Jack reads them when I'm not around. Then Tiny Boy and I would walk northward to the wintering grounds of Maple Jack, Winter Woman, and whoever she serves as healer and shaman.

I've heard from a number of folks that north of the man-made borderlines there are mountains beyond mountains, as far as the eye can take in, vistas unmatched anywhere. I have no desire to do much of anything save see them, for once they are in my mind, they are a part of me, can never leave me.

Jack thinks I'm loco. He doesn't understand why a man would swap the opportunity to while away the cold months snugged in deep with a buxom woman who giggles at everything he says. I find this difficult to believe, and I suspect they don't speak the same tongue. Then again, they are each human and are fond of each other's company, at least for a time, so perhaps that's enough.

I know from what he's told me that by the time the blankets are hopping with bugs and the snow's dripping outside and the mighty sun lingers longer each day, they are looking for excuses to get out of their cozy little nest of love and away from each other. Then there comes a day when the goldfinches are back for the season and the snow's less than more, patched and waning in the sun with each passing moment. That's when they each know, somehow they know, that it's time to part for the year.

He packs and she watches him ride southward aboard Ol' Mossback the mule, and she sighs and drags out the bedding and beats it without mercy, and they each bathe in frigid freshets fresh from the peaks and go on with their own lives, nothing passing between them but thoughts over distance.

Spring becomes summer, and summer gives over to autumn. That, too, comes and then goes. There's a middle to that time, a gap in the calendar when the wind pulls in its hoary breath and there's nothing save silence and stillness and a coldness that hasn't been felt since the year before.

You let out a rattly breath, stuttering with something that's not quite excitement, not quite fear . . . perhaps a little of both. You see your breath's little cloud plume from your face, then the wind does the same back, pushing winter at you, on you, in you. And you had better be where you want to be when that first storm thunders in.

Maple Jack knows this wedge time well, and so does Winter Woman.

CHAPTER FOUR

Six days later, I was once more packed and roving northward, having left Jack's cabin snug and buttoned up for the rest of the cold months, the mice and ermine and snow and wind the only residents hardy enough to live there without flame.

I smelled winter on the air, and though snow had already fallen, melted, and settled a time or two more, the distinctive tang of bone-coldness to come, carried down from on high on winter winds, told me this will be a decision I have to be certain of. There would be little opportunity to return to the lowlands with Tiny Boy once the biggest storms hit in the coming months. No, I am confident in my decision.

Especially so since my last foray into the deep, high mountains a few seasons back, tracking thieves and killers to a standstill, hoping to rescue the woman they'd taken from the train. Had I known how close I would come to death, how close Jack would come, I would have . . . no, that is untrue. I still would have gone, hoping against hope I could save her. Even when I knew I could not, that it was too late. Even when I learned that it had been too late before I began that vicious trek, on foot, punching hole after hole in the blizzard snow, higher, ever higher. I still would have gone, more the fool am I.

I have always loved the mountains. The sight of them from afar is even more impressive close-up, and made better being within them, part of them, as they rise up all about you. I want to embrace the mountains, not avoid them. I know that even

early in the season, the snows on the high-up slopes will already
be deep and hard-going.

That is why back in the summer, Jack sought out his friend,
Little Turnips, a Salish elder, to visit and teach me how to build
my own snowshoes. For me it was not enough to barter for
them, or worse, buy them outright at a mercantile. I felt like I
needed to build my own. Proper snowshoes with bentwood
frames and hide webbing, and sizable enough to keep me from
sinking too deep.

It took the best part of a month, and it worked. I glanced at
them, wagging slightly from their perch strapped on the saddle,
and I felt a flash of smug pride. They were solid, they were large
enough to support me, and I made them, with Little Turnips's
guidance. Yes, they would serve me well in the coming expedition.

Little did I know that the adventure I had planned for myself
would be anything but peaceful and quiet. Had I known, I
would have turned back then and there. That's the thing about
life, isn't it? We never know what lies waiting for us up ahead on
the trail, hidden by that boulder or copse of trees. Waiting,
twitching its tail and breathing shallow, watchful of us as we
stumble forward. Waiting to pounce.

CHAPTER FIVE

It took us five days of steady work to make it to the south end of Salish Lake, the winter stomping grounds of Maple Jack and Winter Woman. I'd pressed it more than I usually do, and I wasn't certain why. As a rule, I don't rush my way through my days. I enjoy my time and try to take in everything I see. This is what's most precious, after all, the time in our days and how we make use of it.

On that fifth day out from Jack's cabin, we crested a rise that afforded me a long view of the vast lake ahead, and a close-in view of the country to come, a long slope that settled into a treed shoreline. I felt a twinge in my gut. It was not due to lack of food, as I'd munched biscuits and jerky and dried apple rings in the last hour. No, this was what Jack calls a "hanty sort of feeling." I have always taken that to mean a haunting of sorts, spooky, unexplained, the sort of feeling that leaves you with goose-fleshed arms and the desire to flee.

All it made me do is hasten forward to find my friend. And I did find him, though not as I had expected to.

I saw what I knew to be Winter Woman's cabin. Had to be. It sat how Jack had described it. A river wound its way north of me, downslope from the same ridge I had crested. The scatter of pines and aspen thickened lower down by the nibble of a clearing where the cabin sat on a small rise overlooking the river, a couple of hundred feet from the lakeshore. I stood still, and so did Tiny Boy, and we eyeballed the slope, appreciating the location she had chosen.

If I could shed my fiddle-footed ways, I figured I could do a whole lot worse than to end up in the trees, close by a river and a lake. I pictured a canoe drawn up on shore, a fishing rod in my hand, and a warm fire puffing out smoke from my stone chimney. That's when I snapped out of my daydream.

I knew what had been nibbling at my guts since I crested the rise. No smoke. It was nippy enough that, though I couldn't see the cabin in full, I could tell from Jack's frequent florid descriptions where it sat. And from that spot, on this nippy day, there should be chimney smoke.

Now that didn't mean something was wrong. They could be away for the day, could be cleaning, who knows? I'm not in the habit of speculating on such thoughts, however. It's a waste of time. What I do know is that I had that feeling worming in my gut, stronger than ever. It was all very odd.

"Come on, boy," I said to the horse, and though I held the reins in my mittened left hand, as soon as I began hoofing it cross-slope downward, he followed along, nimble as a goat. I don't know how he does it, since he's as particular as a stage dancer about where he puts his feet.

As we lost elevation, I also lost sight of the spot where I knew the cabin was. It took a few more minutes of steady arm-swinging walking, my breath rising up into the chill air, the sky far less blue than it had been an hour before.

I take particular care to keep a weather eye. I've been caught unawares in the past as storms moved in. Rain, snow, wind, or a combination of all that results in stinging pellets of ice that will burn and probe you like buckshot from the heavens. And once, some years back, I found myself in a wildfire in Wyoming Territory that pounded forward in a wide front like an orange ocean wave, ravenous in its appetite and unstoppable.

I happened to be afoot at the time and made it to a river as the charred, smoking, wide-eyed beasts I found myself running full bore among all lurched forward into the same flowage. It was the Green River, and at that moment, its coolness was the finest balm I have ever felt or will ever feel.

The river about me was a froth of thrashing, bellowing, screaming creatures, everything from mice and moles and snakes to foxes and wolves and one singe-haired grizzly thrashing his way to the far bank. I didn't have long to think about it. I swiveled my head as if it were on an axle as I made my way downstream, the current doing more for me than my feeble efforts. My buckskins felt heavy, sodden as they were, though they'd stopped smoking. That's a tale for another time, though. Point is, I keep an eye on the weather all the time.

And on that day, the far-off bank of gray cloud, like an old man's furrowed brow, told me something was coming in, something large and distant, yet coming nonetheless.

And I still had that hanty feeling. I hustled along, stamping one boot after another, and made the river, figuring that trekking along its near bank would bring me to the cabin before long. I was right.

We passed through trees, the same I'd seen from above. The aspens were bare of their leaves, but the ponderosas were green and a kindly sight. I take great comfort from trees. They are stalwart and dependable, eminently useful, unlike most humans, me included, and all they ask for in return is to be left alone. Pretty good deal on our part, even if we don't respect their wishes.

I broke through the copse of trees and there was the cabin, close in truth to what Jack had told me it was like. A wide porch—a settin' porch, Jack called it—ran the length of the cabin, perhaps twenty feet long. Like everything else, the cabin was built of logs. Posts held the low porch roof that tapered down to perhaps five and a half feet at the low end.

I assumed that if she was a good fit for Jack, Winter Woman was not very tall. Jack is burly, though he's no giant, maybe three, four inches shy of six feet. I'm a few inches in the other direction, north of six feet. I'd hit my head before the visit was up, that much I knew.

As I walked closer, I slowed my gait. That feeling in my gut was scaling its way up my throat and clanging bells in my skull. Bells of warning. Beyond the cabin sat a small barn, one half of it open faced. Out front sat a corral with its rails burst, as if a mighty wind had scattered them.

This was no longer the tidy cabin and dooryard, as Jack said folks in New England called a front yard, of a tidy woman who prided herself on keeping a tidy place. Her home had been wronged, violated.

Back in front of the house, possessions lay scattered about. Everywhere I looked, I spied something else handmade, now broken, twisted, smashed, tossed, and stomped into the earth. As if a herd of mustangs had barreled through, eyes wide in terror. Except this was no mustang herd. This was the work of two-legged marauders.

How did I know? I saw prints in the dirt, mashed in what must have been a slight patch of mud at the time, from a snowmelt or perhaps a late rainstorm. They come in and are heavy at times. A week or two later and they would be snowstorms.

This was a footprint, a human footprint. A bare human foot. That made no sense, given the season. Yet the oddity of it was the least of my concerns. I kept up my swiveling head habit and, bending low, cat-footed over to the nearest cabin wall, the northwest end.

My Schofield was in my hand, already cocked. I didn't recall cocking it or even freeing it from my holster, and that worried me. For a man who prefers to live the life of a pacifist, I can't seem to get away from guns and the damage they do to another person. Yes, for hunting they're vital, and I value my two guns, my Smith & Wesson Schofield revolver and my Sharps carbine, a heavy rifle and deadly accurate. That's the way I want it when I take down a deer. I want to end its suffering before it begins.

In order for something to live, something must die. Plain and simple. And while I'm alive, other things will die to keep me walking and talking and thinking and reading. It won't always be that way, though. Someday, something will get the better of me and that will be that.

I wanted to shout for Jack, but I'd been in enough dicey spots to know a marauder could still be inside. Or worse, drawing a slight line on me from the trees or the point of land beyond the south end of the cabin. That worrisome thought jerked me tighter to the logs. They'd been stripped of bark with care. I saw the long, even marks of a drawknife. I wondered if Jack had helped her build the place. If so, that's one of the few things he never told me about her.

Jack's a handy fellow when he wants to be. He brought with him a satchel of basic woodworking tools when he ventured West as a younger man, and what he didn't have, he has bought or made since. The workmanship of the furniture in his cabin rivals that of anything you'd find in a fine house in St. Louis.

I paused, leaning against the logs, looking about, knowing every second I waited was a wasted second. I had to find Jack. I reversed course, my back still to the logs, and made it to the corner that led to the rear of the cabin. I bent lower and peered around. Nothing save the jut of stone from the chimney halfway down the wall. I did see two windows, shutters wide open.

I low-walked to the nearest window and peered in. Glass made from bottles filled the gap, with daubing between, securing them in place. I couldn't see through them. The only useful thing such windows do is shed mottled, colored light inside an otherwise dim cabin interior.

I continued on along the long backside of the cabin past the chimney—nobody lurking behind its protrusion—and two steps more brought me to the other window. As with the previous one, the shutters were open, not what I would expect to find if Jack and Winter Woman planned to be gone for more than a day, or even a few hours. The shutters themselves were fastened by stout braided cord that trailed inside the wall through small holes so they could be tugged shut and tied from the inside. A nice idea, useful for keeping harsh weather from pelting the bottle glass, or perhaps repelling attackers if they came from this direction.

I stepped to the end of the building once more and peered around the corner, expecting to hear a loud boom, the last thing I'd ever hear. Nope. Once more luck was with me.

That end, too, was windowless. I crossed it and that brought me to the front of the house again, the low porch roof to my left. The front door was situated on this side of the house, though not centered. I leaned out, first with the snout of the Schofield, then with my own snout. Only that fresh, scattered clutter of possessions greeted me.

I set one boot on the porch, split logs with the flat facing up and planed smooth. More of Jack's handiwork? As soon as I set my second foot, and with it the rest of my bulk, on the puncheons, ducking my head to avoid the supporting cross timber of the porch roof, I heard the floor squeak. Pegged and a little loose by the cold weather, it squawked with each step.

Between me and the door sat a window, this one with two panes of thick, opaque glass. Crossing it would expose me to whoever might be in there. Nothing for it except to rush by and get to that inviting darkness within. The door stood opened inward halfway, a dark angle of unmoving shadow waiting for me.

I made it in one, two steps, and a few more squeaks, and nothing shot at me or leapt out with a knife. I appreciate such moments in life. They give a fellow another reason to walk lively. I'm quite certain Tiny Boy was watching me and wondering what sort of silliness I was up to. He's wiser than me, yet as he didn't offer a better way of going about this, I bulled on in and kicked the door the rest of the way open before ducking low and shunting quick to the left.

I was staring at more mess in what looked to be the main living area. The rafters were hung barely above head height of a short person—well, shorter than me—with drying herbs and flowers, and leaves, what looked like collections of roots, likely for weaving or tincture making or both. In the low light, I saw the maw of the fireplace, cold and black against the center of the back wall. A wide span in the left back corner bore shelves, and below that sat a large worktable, smooth with age and use.

I stepped further to the left while eyeing the dim cabin and found myself in the corner, where I wanted to be in case anyone was in there. I didn't want openness behind me, not if there were folks with ill intent about.

Now I saw in the far rear right corner what I assumed to be a large bed, mounded with quilts and furred skins. The only spot I'd not seen in the cabin was the opposite front corner, the first corner I'd come upon from outside. I bent even lower, trying to avoid getting a face full of dried greenery, and slowly the spot came into view. It was lined with more shelves, and those had apparently been left unmolested, filled with crocks and crates and sacks.

A mouse darted from that front corner as quick as its little legs could work, to the back corner beneath the bed. Of a person, either Jack or Winter Woman or an attacker, there was no sign.

I walked with less reserve now and crossed to the bed, first stopping before the fireplace, where I palmed the ashes, suspecting I'd feel no warmth. I was correct. I moved to the bedside.

There, on the floor at the foot of the bed, was a large parfleche, and beside it a hefty bow-handled cloth bag. Both were Jack's, there was no missing that fancy beadwork adorning the outside of the latter, and the careful, painted decoration of the former. Now that I looked about me, I saw that his possessions, few in number yet important to the man, lay throughout the cabin.

"Jack?" My timid voice cracked the stillness of the cold cabin. "You here?"

Nothing, not even a mouse squeak, greeted my query. I repeated it and was offered the same response.

I walked over to Jack's parfleche and bag and nudged them with my toe, looking over my shoulder up into the dark, cramped rafter space above. I saw no one. I grew bolder and searched faster then, toeing through the storm of items too numerous and tangled to discern what each was, all familiar somehow, common items and scraps of clothing. I saw wooden spoons with their long handles snapped as if in rage, skins with tufts torn out, pegs broken off their nesting places in the walls, and then I saw the one item that made me wince.

It was Jack's stud-handled belt tomahawk and sheath. It's pretty much the first thing he dons in the morning and the last he tugs off at night. He keeps the edge razor keen with a strop that goes everywhere he goes, and rarely have I seen it anywhere but on him. If we're encamped together on the trail, it's piled gently atop other gear, ready for his quick hand to grab. He prefers it for self-defense to what he calls "a fool's reliance" on the bluster and boom of firearms.

He does enjoy hyperbole, though with Jack there's always a niggling sliver of truth of intention behind his bold, broad statements. Not to say he doesn't own a firearm. He does, several, in fact. He is fond of the big, old blunderbuss type of brutes that will dislocate a man's shoulder and make him reconsider most everything he's ever gotten up to in his days on earth. I've had the misfortune to shoot the thing he carries. Its make is a mystery to me, and to him, I suspect. Once pulling its trigger is enough. It's a doozy.

A jumble of ransacked mess is one thing, yet seeing that beloved tomahawk tossed without regard, and not on his person, let me know beyond doubt Jack was in serious trouble. I'd also seen all I needed to see in the house, so I bolted back out the door, swiveling my head once more, seeing nothing I didn't want to see. A glance told me Tiny Boy stood where I'd left him, looking as bored as ever, though perhaps with a faint grin on his mouth.

I made for the stable and, standing to one side, yanked open the door. No sign of Ol' Mossback, or of the donkey Jack had said Winter Woman kept for helping deliver her goods to the scatter of whites and tribes in these hills.

I picked my way fast through the detritus strewn about the dooryard and back to Tiny Boy. I dithered a moment, wondering if I should unburden him of the goods we'd brought along, wondering if I should take him with me, wondering too many things that ended up wasting another half minute of precious time I could spend looking for Jack and the woman.

Finally, I led Tiny to the stable, stripped off his gear, left a hackamore on, and tied him in the widest stall. I borrowed an armload of brittle, gathered grasses and palmed up a scoop of water from the wooden bucket and sniffed it. No off smells— marauders will do funny things, I've found, such as urinating in water supplies, or worse. I dipped my tongue in it—still okay. I left it for Tiny and emerged once more to face the yard. To my right sat the lake, some ways off, yet large and bright, even in the coming cloudiness. I shielded my eyes and saw nothing on its vast surface but trees and rocks along the shoreline. I bent my attentions to the immediate—the yard once more.

My tracking skills pale in comparison with Jack's, though I've gotten better over the years. Not that he'd admit it. Still, I was grateful for the obvious rainstorm they'd had some days before, as the footprints I'd seen earlier, still mystifying when I looked at them again, were imprinted deep. They weren't abnormally large, but they were of human making, and likely a man's, given their wide, burly appearance.

Which tribes were wintering up this way? Likely Salish, and others besides. Barefoot this late? Why not? I didn't know their ways well enough to pass an opinion. I'd met plenty of tribes-men, women, and children who were tough, tougher than I could ever hope to be.

I kept my nose down, eyes wide, ears perked, Schofield in my hand. On my person I had a half-full cartridge belt, and on my right hip, a long knife, thick bladed and wide on the spine for splitting kindling. It's built of bold steel, made by a black smithy in Arizona Territory who never smiled, never made a sound. He stared at me with wet, red eyes as if he'd spent his entire life in the choking smoke of his craft. And I reckon he had.

I had described what I was after, a big knife, I told him as I handed him the sketch I'd made on a thin scrap of backing panel from an old crate.

As I spoke and pointed with my thick fingertip, he nodded. He poked at it a couple of times, too, then looked at me with raised eyebrows.

"Yes, a good guard, brass would be nice. I don't reckon you have such?" I asked.

He'd nodded that he did. A nice surprise. As to the handle, I intended to make that myself while on the trail. I looked forward to it, in fact. I would hew it from some antler I'd saved from a bull elk Jack and I brought down the season before.

"How much?" I'd said.

Without hesitation he looked at me and raised a huge, work-thickened hand, palm toward me, calluses ridging it and his fingers like protruding bone. Five fingers outspread. I waited for him to flash the five once, twice more. He didn't.

"Five dollars?" I said, my eyebrows pinched in question.

He nodded, so I did, too. "Um, how long?"

He looked back over his shoulder at his shop, as if the devil in his forge were beckoning. He glanced beyond me at the sky, then back to my eyes, and held up two fingers.

"Two days?"

He nodded.

"Okay, then. That sounds fine. I'll be back here in two days' time." I held out a hand to shake. "Thanks."

He looked at my hand, then at me, and turned back to his forge. For two days I alternated between feeling excited about having a new knife and curious as to why he'd all but scoffed at my extended hand. I chalked it up to the fact that he'd likely been the target of ill intent by whites most of his life, enough so that he had built up a surly shell as protection, thicker and tougher than his calluses. Or it could have been that reticence I've always encountered when meeting others. I have that sort of face, says Maple Jack. Yes, yes, I do.

As to what I'd need my big hip knife for, I hoped not much, battlewise. After nearly belly-crawling about the place, following stomped footprints and moccasin tracks large and small, which told me Winter Woman and Jack had both fought whoever attacked, I concluded all that nosing about was getting me nowhere.

I began anew, following what tracks trailed away from that clot of muddied confusion before the cabin. Two led me as I followed more of the bare footprints. I'd counted at least three sizes and one who was curiously missing a toe, the second smallest on the right foot. An interesting and potentially useful detail for use in tracking.

The third trail I found was the most promising, for in addition to the prints left by bare feet every now and again, I saw, close to the cabin and leading away with those prints, the smaller moccasin prints, heavy in the heel, then indentations that may have been knees or the heels of a woman's hands. These prints—moccasins and hands—had to be those of Winter Woman.

Perhaps this was where she'd fallen or been pushed or clubbed and dropped. I hated the thought, yet there it was. Then, oddly enough, those tracks disappeared. Then I figured out why: One of the sets of bare feet, where I could still see them, dented deeper, as if burdened. That meant he'd carried Winter Woman. Perhaps after knocking her unconscious. That might mean they'd taken her alive.

This also gave me hope they'd done the same to Jack. My hope was short-lived.

I had already spent a good ten minutes at this and my glances skyward increased. That storm hadn't magically evaporated or moved on in a different direction, but neither was it approaching with any great speed, one saving grace.

Still, if it meant snow, which was likely given the increasing chill of the air, I would lose my opportunity to track them, or at least to decipher a direction to make for. Most men, tracked or otherwise, will blaze a line for home once they've done whatever it is they need to do. Unless they're wily and looking to cover their tracks.

That set of prints led me away from the cabin toward the northwest, into the mountains, far north of where I'd come across the ridge's spine. Trouble was, I found no sign of Jack's big, wide moccasins. Still, I trailed after those tracks for a couple of dozen yards and made note of where I left off, should I get caught up rummaging elsewhere.

Then I went back to the front of the cabin and stared down at the scene with fresher eyes, my arms crossed. I'd holstered the Schofield and now put all my effort into seeing, actually seeing, what I was looking at. It's an art, as Jack has told me in the past, to be able to look deeper, to "get in there with the eyes of a crow."

That's when I saw it. A slight scuff, to be sure. A scuff that looked a whole lot like Jack's scuffing. Wishful thinking on my part, maybe. I made for it, where it peeked out from beneath a welter of crushed and strewn items jumbled to the left side of the low porch step.

I had seen those items earlier, yet in my haste took it to be nothing more than what it appeared, a pile of leavings from the ransacking. Now I toed it, and beneath a wad of pinked-with-age and oft-repaired longhandles I took to be Jack's—he owned two sets—the rest of the moccasin print was revealed, along with a dark patch on the ground.

I held my breath and I touched a finger to it. It was dry, ir-regular in shape, and could be a number of things. No, only one. Blood. I knew it. That it might be Maple Jack's was too soon to tell. I shoved away the rest of the junk and saw droplets making no pattern at all and no more moccasin prints.

"Try, Roamer," I whispered. On my knees, I palmed the dirt and lowered my face even with the ground. Looking across the dark spot, I shuffled, knee-walking toward the cabin, still with my head low, looking in all directions. I even sniffed the spot, and smelled nothing.

It was too cold for me to discern anything more. Then I saw it, as I was about to raise my cheek off the ground. A faint, obvious, irregular line of the moccasin tracks. And closer, between me and the right side of the porch, in among the dried knot of browned grasses, I spied more of the staining. This time it was not merely caked into the dirt. It had been splashed up and down a number of stalks of long, dried grasses. Still dark, yet fading to a deep red at the narrowed edges of the brittle grass.

I sucked in a breath and tried to analyze it critically, as Jack would. This likely meant he'd been clubbed, for the head will bleed quicker and more readily than anything else in the body. The proof becomes clear should you punch someone square on the nose. It will run red nearly every time, and create an enemy who has experienced a wallop of pain. A broken nose is an instant, eye-watering dunk into a pool of agony.

I fancied I saw matted grasses that could well have been where Jack, unconscious, had lain. Perhaps he had tried to save her, they struggled, he was hit, and probably from behind. Maple Jack won't put up with an attack from the front, not without a brutal fight in which he will bite off ears and noses, and gouge eyes. He abides no rules when he's fighting to the death. And he views each fight as having potentially mortal consequences.

I retraced my steps away from the cabin, this time following the vague trail of dark drips, no larger than a tooth, here and there. Thankfully the yard was worn smooth in places and I was amazed to find blood where I had overlooked it before. In some instances, I had stepped on it in my blind haste.

Now I had a direction, a better-painted picture, and a better sense of why. Or so I told myself.

Not knowing what might await me up the trail, I hesitated at the thought of leaving the cabin and Tiny Boy behind. Then I bolted back for the wee stable, untied Tiny's hackamore, and slipped it off his head. If for some reason I did not make it back, he would at least have a chance to survive. "Hope for the best, plan for the worst," as someone wise once said. I bet it was Jack.

I rummaged in my coat pocket, found the cloth-wrapped wad of jerky I kept there, an apple in the other pocket, and decided that would be enough. I had to go. One more glance at the gray sky and I made for the trail, armed with the disturbing vision of the spots of blood that I didn't want to be Jack's.

CHAPTER SIX

I tracked on, bent low and eyeing ahead and side to side for
clues. I was rewarded now and again with bent branches, scuffed
spots in the duff. I saw that the captors, as I thought of them,
took no pains to cover their obvious trail. Perhaps they were
confident of their skills in fighting. Or they did not expect to be
followed. I cursed myself more than once for not taking to the
trail northward sooner. I might have been able to help prevent
whoever it was I was dogging.

Such thoughts are not useful. The past is a dead thing,
unchanging. I reasoned I'd gone more than a half mile from the
cabin when I paused, eyeing the terrain about me. I could barely
hear the river behind me, rushing down to the lake. As rivers go
it wasn't a big one, perhaps a dozen feet across at its widest,
and riffled at times to a fault, revealing more rock than water in
the shallows. It flowed, nonetheless.

I scrambled up, then crested a gray, tumbled mound of small
boulders and surveyed the surrounding scene from my paltry
vista, roughly twice my height. It made all the difference. Not
forty feet away, roughly northwest beyond me, I spied a dark
shape moving. Could be a bear, late season and fed and looking
for a spot to hole up.

Whatever I saw shifted from sight a moment, then back into
view. An animal rocking on its haunches. I bent low again and
tried to keep quiet and see it for what it was. No luck. I retreated
down the boulders, chosen only because they seemed in line

with the scant trail I'd been following, and because the low scrub growth to either side was thicker.

I cut wide, figuring I'd approach it from the west, and tried to keep quiet doing so. It didn't work. I saw the thing, still not moving much, yet it also didn't seem bothered by my branch-snapping self.

As I neared it with slow steps, I weaved my head back and forth like a snake testing the air, and I saw it for what it was, Ol' Mossback. I walked close enough for him to see me, and never have I beheld a sadder sight.

He was scratched from flank to face, raked by branches, no doubt. His lead rope was snagged, wound hard and jerked tight on a fallen tree. Somehow the crazy mule had managed to wrap it several times around two bent, solid, snapped branches. Mired as he was in the puckerbrush and lashed tight by the lead rope, Ol' Mossy wasn't about to go anywhere.

Once more I gave thanks that I hadn't shown up days later or not at all, and instead opted to do what I usually do in wintertime, which is to slowly make my way southwestward to prospect some in Navajo country.

The only thing Mossy seemed able or inclined to move was his head, which he swung toward me. Then he did the same thing he always does when he sees me. He brayed, a chesty rumbly sound that Jack refers to as his "love call." He says Mossy only does it when I come around. One of these days I'm going to tire of Jack's ribbing and cuff him one. I hoped it would be that day.

"Good to see you, too, boy," I said, keeping my voice low, lest someone I didn't want to meet was close by.

I patted his neck and scratched his topknot and rubbed his muzzle while I peered around. "What are you doing out here, pal? And in this fix?"

The mule had been there for some time, perhaps a day or

more, snagged as he was. His wounds were not deep, yet pestery. Had it been hot-weather season, he'd have been plagued by flies. Still, those scratches were bothersome to him, I could tell by the way he kept shivering his withers.

After a vigorous head rubbing, Mossy went back to what he'd been doing before I arrived. He stood lock-kneed, head drooped, and appeared to slip into a doze. I set to work freeing him and soon saw how he'd gotten himself in his woodsy fix.

On his far side, a rough channel of snapped branches revealed his route. "Did you get here alone, Mossy?" Maybe Jack came to and hopped aboard, hoping, no doubt, to gain time on the ruffians who'd dragged his woman off. Then the going got too thick, so instead of backtracking, Jack cut Mossy loose and proceeded on foot himself. It seemed a plausible notion. And yet I know that no matter how riled Jack could get, he wouldn't have left the mule alone out here, at least not with a rope hanging from his jaw.

"Okay, Mossy. Let's go." One of those big ears flicked, so I know he heard me. I proceeded onward, following what I took to be a fresh trail left by someone. I hacked it wider with my big knife, wide enough for the mule, who followed without complaint, at least until I could find a clearing where I'd leave him for a short spell, I hoped. I'd have to get him to water soon.

A hundred or so feet uptrail, the trees thinned and became piney once more. The air was tart, snappy with a freshness to it, and laid over it all like a thick blanket lay a quietness, as if something big had been decided by unseen powers.

I led Mossy to a boulder and leaned against it myself for a moment. If I had to continue bushwhacking, I needed a few moments of fresh breath. Then Mossy bolted around me to the far side of the boulder, braying and snorting. He stopped, head down, snorting up a storm. I followed, figuring he'd found a spring weep hole or something brittle yet toothsome to snack on, at least to him. Never did I think he'd find Maple Jack himself.

CHAPTER SEVEN

The old buck was folded over in a heap of bloody buckskin on the ground. His hat was missing and his long, silvered hair and beard were clotted with thick, dried blood.

I dropped to my knees and laid a hand on his shoulder. His buckskins were cold, but when I squeezed, I felt soft flesh beneath. I gently rolled him onto his back and straightened his legs.

"Jack? Jack?" I patted his cold cheek. "Maple Jack, you wake up!" I said it sterner, swatting his cheek and watching his eyelids. Nothing.

His head was a mess, though the blood had congealed. I held my ear to his mouth and felt breath there. Still, I checked his breathing twice more, once with my hand and again with my ear. Yes, he was breathing. Slight, yet he was alive.

I knew he'd been following the attackers. Yet to do so in that sad a state, clubbed and left for dead, I presumed, was not something Jack would try. At least not in his right mind. No matter how bad a situation seemed, he always emphasized taking a moment to think, then outfit yourself as if you were going into a battle you might not win if you didn't think ahead first.

That told me he *wasn't* in his right mind. He'd likely come to in a heap by the cabin steps, addled and bloodied. He'd had enough mental capacity, though, to follow their trail. Maybe he'd seen which direction they'd been headed before he faded out.

All this was speculation that could wait.

"Mossy, you deserve a medal, fellow. Before we celebrate, we have to get Jack to the cabin." I hoped there wasn't anything pierced inside, nor bones broken. I had to get him up on Mossy's back. I bent low, lifted him as a parent will a sleeping child, and was surprised how light he felt. On his two feet, and with a snootful of his "squeezin's," as he calls them, Jack is a formidable presence, but I reckon a clubbing and no sustenance for who knew how long—a day? two?—was rough enough treatment to whittle him down to a hollowed version of himself.

"We'll get you back in form in no time, Jack," I said. I wanted to carry him, as I thought that might prove less of a jostling journey and I did not know if he was injured inside, nor how extensive his wounds, inside and out, were. Though he felt light to me, and though my large size was a useful trait in this situation, I was worried I'd tire out far too soon and have to stop frequently. I needed to get him back to the cabin as quickly as I could.

I decided to try to keep him atop Mossy for as long as I was able. I'd carry him as a last option. And it would have to be as one would a child—before me, not over the shoulder. That would be far too rough, even for as tough an old cob as Maple Jack.

It didn't take long to load him up. It was a trick to keep him upright on Mossy's back. Disgusted with myself for propping and jostling my poor, unconscious mentor in such a manner, with me walking on Mossy's left side, and Jack sagged against my hands, we made our way back down the trail that wasn't a trail.

If Mossy felt fresh pain from the walk or the grasping branches, he didn't show it. And what's more, that mule didn't need me to lead him. He knew where he needed to get to and wasted no time in retracing the route back to the cabin.

Winter Woman would have to wait. It may sound callous, but Maple Jack was my first concern. With him revived, if that was possible, too early to tell, I might be able to glean information from him about the attackers.

I was heartened by the fact that Jack's breathing—I gave Mossy a "whoa, whoa now" every so often, to check on Jack— sounded steady. Under my palm his chest worked with regular effort. I listened closely and heard no rattles as he inhaled and exhaled. I'd heard plenty of folks breathing a trembly sound through strings of blood and phlegm clogging and filling their lungs and windpipes. So far, Jack was pulling in the right direction.

The only time Mossy faltered on me was when we came within sight of the river. He kicked up his effort into a trot. I had the lead line loosely wrapped in my left hand, should I need to steer him or slow him, though mostly so it wouldn't snag on another bramble patch. The water teased that parched poor mule and the rope whipped from my grasp.

In his lust for a drink, Mossy forgot his task of ferrying the one he was most devoted to. He stumbled, and I had to grab Jack's crusty buckskin tunic and pull him toward me as the mule's front right leg buckled beneath him.

He went down on that knee, and Jack flopped over onto me. Trying to maintain my stance, I lashed out with my left hand, losing my grasp on Jack's torso. I staggered backward and slammed into a ponderosa that would have felt far less painful were it not for the jagged nubs of snapped branches.

I thought for a moment I'd been pierced through. But I felt no wetness seeping in, and reckoned my thick wool coat was armor enough. I managed to keep Jack from flopping to the ground and hefted him higher, cradling him once more.

By then, Mossy was back on all four hooves and showed no remorse for his ill treatment of us. He continued on to the river, ambling, not limping, and waded right into the flow. His head was down and drinking even before his muzzle touched the cool water. I felt bad for the old gent—he'd been fetched in the trees for how long, only he knew. He was as parched as if he had been wandering the Mojave.

As the cabin was close by, not yet in sight, though I would soon see it, I figured I'd carry Jack the rest of the way. Mossy would have to make his own way back. If not, I'd scout him up later.

This time crossing the river I wasn't choosy, toe-dancing from rock to boulder to wobbly stone to make the far bank without wet feet. Jack's bulk had me off-kilter, so I bulled ahead and splashed across the river. I was relieved not to feel any of the icy water slop over the tops of my stovepipe boots. I keep them greased and rubbed enough that I figured I might get through it without damp socks. By the time I reached the far bank I was feeling smug. I angled left, toward a low divot, and stepped where I thought it looked solid. I was wrong.

I sank in on that forward foot, and my right leg kept going. I drove down hard onto my knees. The right kneecap found a knobby little rock and then rolled off it. Oh, it brought quick tears to my eyes and I groaned, but I didn't drop Jack. It took a moment for me to drag my left leg up, bent enough to lever myself back to my feet. It was shaky, but it worked.

How could I ever have thought he was light? "Jack, we get through this, we're going to have to talk. You need to back off the fried beaver meat and pemmican."

I struggled onward, wetness creeping into my left boot. I fancy I heard Jack chuckle, so much so that I glanced at his face. No, it was still sagged and gray. We made it to the cabin without any more commotion. Wedging Jack between the wall and myself, I reached down, thumbed the wooden latch, and kicked the door inward. No shots greeted us, nothing except the same jumbled mess I'd left hours before.

I hoped Tiny Boy was faring well in the stable. Knowing him, he'd eaten everything he could find and then dozed in place, the evidence sticking to his lips and hanging from his mouth.

The sag-rope bed in the far corner was starting to look good. It was Jack who needed it. I laid him on the pile of blankets and swept the rest of the mess to the floor. I'd sort and clean and repair later. First, I had to make certain he was comfortable. Then I had to dipper him up a drink of water, then start a fire and make this cabin habitable again.

Sometime in there I heard a noise outside and spun, keeping low. I slid out the Schofield, thumbing back the hammer and making for the door. I came up on it from the frame side, the frame being thicker than the door's planking, and popped it open. I peered out through the gap and saw nothing, save for a flap of red cloth wagging in a ground breeze.

I edged the door open wider with the pistol's barrel. It squeaked slow and long. I held my breath. No shots came ripping in. I heard steps dragging in the dirt. I edged the door wider and that's when I saw him. Ol' Mossback had made it to the cabin from the river. Good. I'd tie him later.

After I warmed the cabin from the fire, and heated a pot of water I'd fetched from the river, I was able to check Jack over for anything I may have missed. I tore up some sort of cloth I found on the floor that may have been a lady's undergarments and made clean bandages. Then, with warm water and one of the cloth strips, I gently washed Jack's head.

His frenzied hair made it tough going. I kept at it, dabbing and wiping. I had to empty the wooden bowl twice, filling it up with clean water, before his head began to look more like the hairy head of a grizzled mountain goat than the bloody stump it was.

Winter Woman—I'd begun thinking of her as a plump thing

in a buckskin dress, long gray-black hair and apple-like cheeks and sharp eyes that took in all Jack's bluster and knew the man behind them—had a cabin full of tinctures and remedies. I hunted among the pots and jars until I found one that contained what I knew to be some form of bear grease, a healing salve that smelled a whole lot better than any I'd ever been dosed with.

I tested it on the back of my hand in case it contained some form of sizzling hellfire that burned the skin and made the wearer holler. It only radiated a cooling feeling and left me thinking pleasant thoughts about it. I dabbed some on Jack's head, then set the pot of it on the table to use on Mossy's wounds later.

I tugged aside the blankets I'd laid atop Jack. His moccasins were nearly shredded through. I could see the bottoms of his old, hard-as-horn feet through holes in the leather and through the wool socks within. Those feet also reeked now that he was warming. They exuded a mixture of the heady tang of blood and mud and whatever else he had stumbled through, perhaps the fresh, green leavings of deer or some other forest beast.

I untied the rest of the moccasins and peeled off the husks that had once been wool socks. I was tempted to toss them in the fire, yet was afraid what sort of stink they'd fill the house with, and also, they weren't mine to do away with. They were Jack's, and odd as it sounds, it felt like if I tossed them away, he might somehow go with them. It's a silly notion, yet sometimes those are all we have.

His right foot was in bad shape. Black and purple blotches stained his skin, which was swelled around the ankle as big as my clenched fist. No wonder he'd not gotten far. That ankle looked to have been stomped on by a mule. Maybe in his addle-pated state he'd gotten in Mossy's path. Whatever the cause, the foot was in a bad condition, perhaps even broken. I decided to leave it alone for the time being. There wasn't much I could do about it anyway.

I spooned more fire-warmed water into his mouth. I was fast losing daylight, so I secured Jack tight in his blankets once more, then went out to retrieve what few goods I had brought with me. I also wanted to make certain Tiny and Mossy were in the stable for the night. Then I had to finish tidying up the place, inside and out.

Though the woodbox beside the fireplace was full, it wouldn't be enough to keep Jack from slipping into a full-bore case of the teeth-rattling shivers throughout the night. After I dumped my third armload of firewood from the knocked-over stacks out front, I managed somehow to rouse Jack from whatever place he'd been visiting deep in his own head. It wasn't the Jack I knew who came back.

CHAPTER EIGHT

He began with a harsh pull of breath, which he let out with a wheeze. At that point I spun around from hanging bunches of herbs that looked to have been yanked down from the ceiling rafters. His eyes popped open and they were wide, wide and white, blasted through with red veins that looked like he was about to weep a mighty stream of blood.

His mouth worked open, tall and wide like a banked fish will do, then he howled, a ragged breathy sound that goose-fleshed my arms and made my neck hairs stipple outward. He kept at it even as I sat beside him and tried to hush him like a mama will do to a child wakened from a bad dream.

"It's okay, Jack!" I said in a voice I hoped was kind and familiar. "It's all right now, Jack. You're safe now."

Jack looked at me and his wide eyes went wider, and he cackled and shouted sounds that were not words, raw sounds of animal fear. He shrank away from me, shaking his head so fast it appeared he was palsied. "Devils! Devils!"

Those were his first real words, then they trailed off into fearful sounds once more. He scooched back into the corner, churning the covers off him with his feet. He kicked outward and his hands clawed the air. He gripped the blankets in his fists, then unclenched them and caressed the opposite arms.

I repeated my meaningless words. They had no effect on the man. I didn't know what to do with him, and wondered if I might have to strap him down. I couldn't leave him like this, and I didn't know if he was awake or in the midst of a bad dream. I have read of people walking in their sleep, their eyes are open, and they perform all manner of ordinary tasks they might get up to in their wakeful hours. Somnambulism, they call it. I hoped that was the case with Jack, as he seemed fully awake to me.

I took cold comfort in the fact that he had come back to life, though to what extent I didn't quite know. His eyes were odd, bulging, and, well, odd looking. I took that to be because of the knock to his head. It must have rattled his brain.

As I watched him mumbling and moaning and saying words that weren't words, and looking all around him and not seeing anything at all, I wondered if this was Maple Jack from here on out.

As quick as that fearful thought flitted into my mind, I nodded. *Well, Roamer, so be it. He saved your ugly, undeserving hide more than one time. He even tugged you from that blizzard and named you on that cold Christmas Eve all those years before. Least you can do is take care of your friend in his days of need.*

That wasn't the part that bothered me. The part that was worrisome was how I was going to go about doing that.

I figured I had a little time while he was wedged into the corner atop the bed, so I had best make use of it. I moved quietly, and while he turned his head in my direction, he didn't appear to actually see me. His eyes skittered past me, left, right, like two acorns loose in their shells.

I moved slowly across the room and laid more wood on the fire, keeping an eye on Jack. He wouldn't get far with that bum ankle, and I bet his head would be aching something fierce. Yet he was mumbling and wobbling his poor head as if he were a wet dog shaking off water after a swim.

I looked about the dim cabin, wondering what I could do. Winter Woman was a healer, a medicine woman. Maybe some of those herbs I'd picked off the floor and strung back up on the ceiling beams would help him. I know something of herbs and various remedies, though only enough to make simple poultices. I wasn't certain what to do with a madman.

No, Roamer, I told myself, nearly out loud. *Don't talk that way. Jack's not a madman. He's had a bad knock. He'll come around. He's sore in the head.* These types of injuries can take a while to heal. Weeks, maybe months, I don't know.

I wished I'd thought to take my own volume of medicinal advice off my bookshelf at Jack's cabin. It was still there, with all the other books, stories that felt foolish to me then as I sat there feeling close to helpless.

In my tidying, I'd not seen any such books or scraps of writing in the woman's cabin, nothing that indicated she was literate. Of course, she'd have her tinctures and techniques, her cures and time-tested methods secure in her own mind, not written down. I gazed at the plants, dried and so different, withered from their fulsome, summer selves, hanging all about me, my face nearly in them, since the ceiling was rather low.

Then I got a whiff of one, and as the mind will do, it tapped another memory, something faint, something I was unaware of, hidden away like a squirrel's nut in my thinker, as Jack calls it. That, in turn, tapped another, and before I knew it, a trail of thoughts led me to one that might be useful.

"Hello there," I whispered, reaching for the plant. "Are you snooze weed?" I lifted the dried wad down from the hook. I never learned the proper name, but snooze weed was appropriate enough.

The leaves were still attached to their stems, and bound at the base with coarse twine. I brought them to my nose. I sniffed and smelled summer, to be sure, when sunlight pops plants wide, and with their awakening, scents rise so heady I sometimes can hardly believe I prefer winter's bleakness.

"Yes," I said, sniffing again. "Yes, you are." Snooze weed, I recalled, has, among other attributes, an uncanny ability to act as a calmative.

Without waiting another second, I stripped off some of the leaves into a wooden cup, then I dithered and stripped off more leaves. Then a few more, for good measure. I dippered hot water into the cup, stirred it with a stem, and covered it with a small bowl, letting the steam curl back in on what I hoped would be a brew to induce sleep in my wild-eyed friend. Now I had to figure out how to get him to drink it.

Turns out it wasn't that difficult. I'd forgotten that even in his addled state he was mighty thirsty from his ordeal. The animal self inside him sniffed the aroma of the steeped tea and liked it. He leaned forward, his eyes still wild and skittery, still not, now that I was able to see him up close again, able to focus on any one thing.

He snatched at the cup and I held it by the base while his hands trembled and shook and he guzzled the hot liquid down. I winced and hoped I'd not made it too hot, else his lips and gullet would blister. He didn't seem to care.

I was about to pull the cup away, but he kept it gripped close and I saw he was licking the inside of the cup. "Jack," I whispered, "I'll get you more. I won't let you go thirsty, old friend."

He didn't seem to hear me. When I pulled it from him, he shoved back into the corner again, cowering, his hands held before him as if to push away something frightening that was approaching.

I brought the cup back to the water bucket, dippered hot water from the iron pot, then some from the cold bucket, and noticed the leaves were gone from the cup. He'd eaten them. I brought him another drink. Though he took the filled cup from me, he didn't finish this one.

Within minutes he was asleep. I watched as it happened. His head began to jerk less and less, his eyelids fluttered slowly, and the eyes themselves ceased their rattling back and forth.

Finally, his hands unclenched and within another minute he was sagged in the corner, his chin on his chest, snoring like he'd been pole-axed. Those white bandages swaddling his head topped him like a dollop of whipped cream on a knotty chunk of firewood. If I didn't know how ill and injured he was, I'd think him comical.

I waited out the best part of an hour, watching him, checking that he was breathing. I wanted to rearrange him such that he would sleep in a less awkward manner, yet what if he woke? That decided it for me. Until I figured out what I'd been left with—a gibbering friend who needed all manner of attention or someone who needed time to heal up—caution and quiet was the best solution.

I left Jack snoring in a deep slumber, thanks to the snooze weed. I didn't know how long he'd be out. I knew I had to scout the region once more before the storm for sign of the woman's captors, and to reestablish the direction they'd been headed in. That Jack had been on the correct trail when I found him, I didn't doubt. I wouldn't mind gathering proof and further clues before the storm hit.

By then darkness had begun, dusk giving way to a long run of late-autumn hours. I brought more wood inside, then roved the yard, then back uptrail a ways, a fool's errand since I could barely make out my own big feet beneath me. I stumbled back to the cabin's clearing and set up Tiny Boy and Mossy for the night.

I'd sleep fast, as Jack said, then get up before light, make coffee, dose Maple Jack if I could, and get out there. I figured I could cover the distance to where I'd found Jack from the cabin in a sliver of the time I'd done it before.

CHAPTER NINE

I woke early, before light, and made coffee for myself, and tea for Jack. He was still snoozing like a baby, so I took that as a sign. I left the covered teacup beside the bed, within sight and reach, and headed for the hills.

All my meager tracking efforts once more pointed in that direction, which helped me not to waste time. I smelled snow on the air, and despite knowing this, I found myself stopping every so often to sniff like a big boar grizz. Nothing changed from sniff break to sniff break. It was cold, colder it seemed with each passing minute. It was the sort of pinching, dry coldness that presages a big blizzard. I needed to cover as much ground as I could to establish a direction.

As much as I didn't like the idea of abandoning Winter Woman to her fate among the heathens who snatched her, I am beholden to Jack for so much and I couldn't leave him in his sorry state. He'd likely try to crawl on out of the cabin and freeze to death in the snow before I got half a day's journey from the place.

Neither did I like the idea of not helping Winter Woman. It was a devil of a spot to be in—no rights and no wrongs. And no matter what went wrong, I'd be blamed. At least by myself.

I stopped for a breather by a stunty pine growing hard by a granite boulder that had seen a good many storms. It would no doubt sit in that very spot long after man's greedy claw hold had loosened and fallen away from the face of the earth.

I squinted back behind me, downslope and to the southeast. I figured I was a good four, maybe five miles from the cabin. I swung my gaze back northward. The trail had thus far cut fairly true, as if whoever made it didn't care if they were being followed. Or didn't believe they would be. Now and again, I was rewarded with a few glimpses of raw tracks in soft spots, in sand, mud, and streamside soil. I saw again the marks of bare feet—a rounded dent left by a heel, tiny berms where grasping toes had shoved forward, northward.

As I gazed at the mountains beyond me, what I could see of them, anyway—the gray, dense storm clouds had continued to pile up and churn downward, closer with each hour—it became obvious that the folks who'd nabbed Winter Woman and clubbed my friend were headed into the mountains. I wasn't prepared to go there yet. Any daydreams I'd had of finding her tumbling back this way, unhurt and bent on getting home, were only that, dreams.

I had to get back before the storm hit. Plenty to do to keep safe and get Jack back to health. I turned and retraced my route.

Two hours later saw me once more back at the cabin. I glanced about for sign of intruders, saw none, and cursed myself for not setting up some way to warn me, maybe something they would have to move in order to gain entry to the cabin through the door.

The stable looked untouched. I'd check on the two animals later. I wondered again what had happened to the woman's donkey. I'd not seen hoofprints left by a donkey anywhere about the place, and certainly none on the trail to indicate they'd taken the critter as well. I repeated my cautious entry to the dark interior of the cabin as I had the day before. I needn't have.

There was Maple Jack, much as I had left him earlier, propped on the bed in the corner, snoring like a drunken sailor sleeping off a spree. I glanced at the rafters—plenty of snooze weed left. The day's light was still out there, though it was losing its lifelong battle with the man in the moon.

Judging from the amount of wood stacked on the porch and close by the house, I figured Jack had been busy laying in firewood since he arrived. Good thing, as I brought inside as much of it as I could fit. Unfortunately, there was very little meat. I wasn't prepared for that. I had assumed Winter Woman kept a store of dried meat in a cache out back. I saw none. Maybe she ate little meat and obtained her health through trade goods, though for someone who was independent, that seemed unlikely.

Depending on the duration of the storm, I might have to hunt up a deer to get us through the long taper of shut-in time that blizzards leave behind. The stable was easy to button up, having doors to the two stalls. I lugged in extra water from the river, it being closer than the lake. Then I loaded the racks with the gathered dried grasses she or Jack had stored in a lean-to off the side of the stable.

Mossy and Tiny knew each other well and there was plenty of room for them. My thoughts once more turned to the donkey. Perhaps he'd died over the long summer. Time would tell.

I'd brought in the last of my own modest, solid batch of supplies and laid them out on the table. Flour and cornmeal and coffee, tea and dried beans and a small sack of boiled sweets. Even a jug of store-bought whiskey for Jack. I'd save that for later. And neatly wrapped in canvas, that fine, new-to-me copy of Whitman's *Leaves of Grass*. I'd been looking forward to savoring its hidden wonders and had almost unwrapped it once on the trail here.

Fortunately, other tasks had kept me from tucking into the book. If I had sampled it on the trail, I likely would have lingered longer at Jack's cabin, savoring the words, and then where would

Jack be? That thought didn't bear more of my time. Whitman would have to wait for my return. If . . . no, Roamer, I told myself. When I returned.

I looked about the place. The critters were snug in the stable, the outside had been cleaned up, all the scattered possessions brought in and tidied to the best of my ability, and wood and water fetched. I'd hunt up meat when I could after the storm. For now, though, I set to making corn cakes and coffee. And I watched Maple Jack and waited.

All the while, the wind increased and the shutters rattled—I closed them—and the door rattled—I stuffed the bottom gap with rags—and I waited, listening to the storm build itself up into a mighty rager. And I tried not to think about what the future held for any of us.

CHAPTER TEN

Some time in the small hours, that creeping time between midnight and dawn, a lull between rattling blows of the storm woke me. Funny how I could doze among the worst sounds, yet silence pulled me awake. Through years of sleeping on the trail, in dicey regions and safe, none safer than out amongst creatures of the wild as opposed to the tame beasts that populate towns, I've learned to open my eyes before moving.

It's rare that I will jerk awake or make a sound to give away my location. Of course, that wonderful bit of self training and theory powders in the breeze when you consider I've been told by Maple Jack that I snore like a bull grizz. So much for silence.

I looked about the room, not moving from my bundled-up spot in the low, wooden chair before the fireplace. My legs were outstretched, my boots stood leaning like exhausted soldiers, and I wore two pair of wool socks, the holes misaligned on each to cover most of my feet, with my camp moccasins over those. Still, it was cold in there. The fire I saw still bore the faint glow of coals that I would quickly revive.

I listened a moment before I rose from the chair. The storm still buffeted high up in the trees, and I knew it was far from over. The old blue lord of the skies had merely pulled in a great draught of air and was fixing to push it all out on us again. Any time now.

"Hello? Who's there?"

I spun my head toward the dark corner where the bed and

Jack lay. I'd stretched him out and bundled him in blankets many hours since. The voice was old, brittle, dry, not Jack's at all.

"Jack?" I pushed up out of the chair and brought the lantern with me as I half stumbled over to the bed. "Jack?"

"Roamer? Roamer, it's you. Good, good."

"Jack?" I leaned close to his face and looked at him.

He squinted and moved his head away. "What are you doing?" he whispered.

"You're back? You're okay?"

"Well . . ." He tried to smile. "If I look as bad as I feel, then no, I would say I am not okay." His voice sounded wavery, old.

"Would you like a drink of water?"

He looked up at me and seemed to brighten. "You bet."

"Okay," I said, standing up. "Don't go anywhere." If my paltry attempt at humor tickled him, he didn't let on. He sagged in the corner, looking in the dim light as if he'd been deflated, a husk of the man I knew. He was back, though, and sounded, if not in fine fettle, better than he had yesterday.

I filled the dipper from the water bucket, then dumped it back in and brought the bucket and a tin cup over to the bed. He filled the cup and sucked it down, then held it out toward me in a shaky hand.

"We should make sure you don't drink too fast or too much."

"Okay . . . Mama." He tried to smile. Jack was in there after all.

He drank down two more cups and dribbled the last bit down his chin hairs into his matted beard. Then he leaned back, breathing hard from the exertion.

After he caught his breath, he leaned his head back into the corner, wincing as he set it softly against the logs. "What happened?" he asked. He kept his eyes closed.

For a moment I didn't know what to say. I almost spoke,

then I stopped and reconsidered. He'd asked my opening question. Something told me to be cautious. When I opened my mouth to speak, he said, "Where am I?"

Uh-oh. His knock to the head was a corker. At least he knew who I was.

"You've taken a knock to your head, Jack. What's the last thing you recall?"

"Ohhh." He let out a long breath as if he was exhausted, which I've no doubt he was. "Let's see. I was out fetching wood. Winter Woman was waiting dinner on me . . . Is that where I am? Yes." He lifted his left arm and touched the rough log wall. I noticed his fingers still trembled.

"Yes, you're here, at her cabin."

"Where is she? Hey, why are you here? Where has she gone?" His words were bolder than his effort, for his voice was still barely above a whisper. He'd opened his eyes and was looking at me.

"She's . . . not here right now, Jack. She left for a little while."

"What? It smells like snow. I hear wind . . ."

I nodded. "There's a bit of a blow out there now. It'll pass."

"But . . ." He began to breathe harder and his eyes, which had been half lidded like a dozy dog's in the sun, widened. "But . . . no, no!"

He shoved forward, winced with the effort, and held his head with both hands. He sat like that, leaning toward me, his eyes scrunched shut, his breath coming hard through his nostrils. I was worried I was in for another round of the earlier madness I'd seen. Maybe I could stave it off somehow. I laid a hand on the blanket, his leg beneath.

"Jack. It's going to be okay."

"No, no it's not," he said, his voice tight now, no longer a pained whisper. He snapped open his eyes and stared at me. "Don't you see? They took her! Those devils took her!"

Okay, now he was remembering some amount of what happened. "Jack, what devils? Who took her? What tribe?"

"Tribe? No, no, boy, no tribe—they're devils, I tell you!"

"Jack, calm down, you'll hurt your head worse than it is."

I didn't have to tell him that. He was thumbing his temples hard, and his breathing hadn't slowed. "Devils, Roamer! No lie! Those red-eyed cannibals come out of nowhere, howling and shrieking. They were in here when I come up on the porch with my arms full of wood. 'Smells good, woman!' I said to her. My gut was growling because she can cook mighty fine, though I don't mind saying to you I believe I'm her better at certain dishes."

Now this was the Jack I knew. If I didn't know better, if I didn't know his head was a cracked egg and his ankle and foot a puffed mess, I'd think he was his old raconteur self again.

"I nudged open the cabin door with my toe and that's when I saw three of the devils holding her! One on each side, one behind. He had his blood-black bony hands wrapped over her mouth, one hand covered her entire face! She stared right at me over his fingers, a big thumb betwixt her eyes!

" 'No!' I shouted. 'What's this?' I shoved that wood at them, knowing it might hit her, too. I had to do something. That was distraction enough. I went for my 'hawk, but the one in the middle, behind her, he made a deep, growly sound in a voice that never knew human words, and he glared at me. So help me, his eyes glowed red. Red, I tell you! Them other two did the same!

"Winter Woman bucked and thrashed, but they held her tight and made their howly sort of sounds. Their hair was long and hung every which way in greasy ropes, like some tribes will do. They were not of those people. Their hair was matted with blood, as if they washed in it. And they give off a powerful stink. God-awful, Roamer! Oh, it's not something a man can describe, not a skunk smell nor a ten-day corpse, worse and . . . different somehow.

"We'd come to an impasse, something I knew enough of, having been in a hundred and more Injun fights, but nothing like this. You see, they aren't human, Roamer. That's the thing."

I must have looked doubtful at him, because he said, "No, no, it's true, I tell you! As soon as I saw them, I knew what they were, for it's something Winter Woman told me about, something she'd told me not but three days ago. Told me they were watching her from the woods, the devils! Blood devils, spirits that come in before the wind and take what they want. And all they want is people. I expect they've eaten her by now, oh, that can't be . . . can't be . . . ."

"Eaten her? Jack, you're talking crazy now. If that were the case, wouldn't they have eaten you, too? You've got that reserve flesh you're always talking about." I paused, hoping he'd cackle at me like the old Maple Jack. All he did was shake his head, so I continued.

"I tracked them as far as I could get before the storm, that's how come I found you. I think she's alive. I think they took her somewhere with them for a reason, Jack. She's alive, I'd bet good money on it."

"Don't tease me, boy," he said.

"I wouldn't do that, Jack. What you're talking about, that's an old Indian tale, I've heard something similar. That's a tribal ghost story, nothing more."

"No, sir! I seen them, Roamer! They're real, they're alive and they took Winter Woman!"

"They probably need her. You said she's a medicine woman, an herbalist. They need her help somehow, I'm guessing. Otherwise, why would they leave everything behind that they could have sold for money or used as trade goods?"

He didn't say anything. He was far from convinced. I plowed

on. "They clubbed you on the head, Jack, likely left you for dead or maybe they were trying to slow you down. They're not devils. Maybe they're smelly and frightening looking, but what you're thinking they are and what they really are can't work. I tell you, Jack, it's something out of an old Indian tale."

"No, sir!" He shoved forward again, this time not caring that he was splitting his own head, and mine too, with his shouting. "They're barely human, I tell you! I knowed for years they're up here somewhere, didn't know they were up this-a-ways . . . ."

He sagged back and rubbed his head, his breathing hard, his chest working up and down. I decided not to interrupt him again, as it only seemed to make him more riled up.

"They're the Alooknok, and they live in caves deep in the mountains. And they're not human. Not even half a human. Been bred right out of them, if they started out that way to begin with. From what I've heard, they are spawn from the very guts of the earth itself, the boiling pits of hell coughed them up, like diseased spittle! Has to be the case, Roamer, else how could they control the weather like they do? You explain this storm to me, eh, boy? Convenient that it washed away all sign of them, huh?"

He offered a wry grin as if he'd proven an irrefutable point. I still said nothing. Let him steam on. He'd exhaust himself soon.

"It ain't only the weather, neither. It's waterways, they can change the course of a river like that!" He tried to snap his fingers, but his hands were too bruised and cut up. He didn't seem to care, so possessed was he, and he kept right on ranting.

"Animals, too, they can control the thoughts of critters. Course, that goes the same for holding sway over people's thinking." He shook his head. "Didn't get to me that way because I have a strong mind, but Winter Woman, she's very kind, very trusting. Always wanting to help people. Nothing I say makes her change her mind about such things. I reckon that's what

73

makes her *her*, though."

He flashed his eyes on me and almost smiled. "First light, we'll head out together. You and me, that's about how we operate best anyways, eh, Roamer? We'll track her, then lay those devils low. I don't know how. We have to do it, Roamer. Have to!"

He seemed to be simmering down. Jack's one of the least crazy people I know, so if he thinks he saw something that can't possibly exist, I credit it to the fact that he took a mighty knock to the bean. Time would heal him. And a whole lot of gentle rest.

Me, I'm not prone to believing in fairy stories. I wasn't about to argue that point with him. He knew it anyway, yet in his present condition, it would do no good. What I knew was that my best friend, Maple Jack, was addled and raving, his Winter Woman was snatched and dragged off by at least three, likely four or five, barefooted "devils," and there was a blizzard raging outside that would prevent me from doing much of anything for anyone but Jack.

I'd guessed the storm would last all the coming day. I've been through enough of them, I knew it wasn't likely to be a one-nighter. And even when it ended, I had no idea what I was going to do. Get Jack someplace where we'd find help? Go off after the woman? Hunker in there and nurse Jack back to health, enduring what would probably be his growing wrath with me, day by day?

What I needed was time to think. Then a thought brightened my dismal mood. "I'll make some tea, then we can figure out what to do. Okay, Jack?"

"Yeah, yeah, good. I have some idea of where they took her. Up into the mountains north of here. I got me an idea . . ." He sank back, muttering to himself, his mind working over the problem like an old hound on a knuckle bone.

I made a couple of cups of stiff tea. One for him, and one for me. His was . . . greener than mine. I didn't have time for sleep. Too much to do.

CHAPTER ELEVEN

By the time I brought the tea back over to the bed, Jack was deep asleep. I was grateful. Maybe he would rest until daylight. I'm not certain why I thought that. Somehow dawn seems a better time to make decisions, as if you've put behind you whatever devilment pads up to your back in the wee, dank hours and breathes down your shirt collar.

It would give me time to think.

I know my friend, and I know there's no way once he woke that he was going to let me persuade him to stay behind while I went off searching for Winter Woman. No way. Jack had a bad injury to his head, he was dizzy, that was as plain as the homely on my face, and he couldn't walk a step with that gimpy ankle of his. But none of that would stop him, I knew it. He'd bull ahead and then I'd be stuck with having to care for him in deep snow far into the mountains. So I waited him out and used the time to come up with a plan. I tried to, anyway.

I knew when he woke up, he'd be thirsty. He had to be drier than a man ought to be. I guessed as much, anyway, since he hadn't peed at all. So when he woke I was going to dose him with the special-tincture tea once more. He'd argue with me about going out together. I've never lied to Jack before, not in any way that would harm him, and I was going to have to do that in a grand way.

I didn't like how it made me feel, but I had no choice. Having him along would get us both killed, and Winter Woman, too.

But I was up against it. I'd have to lie to him, promise him we'd be roaring to go, then dose him with the tea and leave him behind. Then I'd have to make snowshoe tracks hard and fast on out of there.

I readied my gear, piled what I could without waking him in the far corner of the cabin, and covered it over with the thin blanket I'd worn in the chair. I wondered which Jack would greet me when he woke—the stodgy, defensive Maple Jack or the fun Jack.

He never made it to dawn. He woke after an hour and a half. Despite feeling like a traitor to my friend for what I was about to do, I went on with it.

"What are you doing?" he said in the darkness. The storm had risen out of its lull and was whipping the house with intermittent lashings of wind and pelting snow.

"Oh, good," I said. "You're awake. I'm getting everything ready."

"I know what you're thinking," he said, his hoarse voice still barely more than a whisper. "But you don't have to worry about me. I'll keep up."

"Good to hear it. Didn't think otherwise." I poured hot water over a fresh cup of tea leaves. A whole lot of tea leaves. Tripled the first dose I gave him. I figured that would give me enough time to get well away before he woke again. Trouble was, I was going to leave him in a bad situation, but I had no choice.

I'd already filled the house with wood and stockpiled food atop the table and more by the bed, three buckets of water beside that. A couple of empty buckets, too, for other necessities. Clothes, more blankets, everything I could think of so he'd hopefully be okay.

Normally I wouldn't leave a man as run-down as Jack to fend for himself, but I know him and he'd give me nothing but trouble and pester me. I had to make a start. I counted on his peppery, if diminished, personality to pull him through.

I carried two cups of tea over and sat down on the edge of the bed. "We'll leave at first light. I make that another hour or so. Storm sounds like it's losing its teeth, too, so that'll stand us well." I sipped and glanced at him over the rim of the cup.

He sipped hungrily, greedily, once the not-too-hot water touched his lips. He finished the cupful. "What is this?" he said, dragging the back of a hand across the dribbles on his chin hairs and chewing through the mouthful of soggy leaves I'd stuffed in the cup.

"A type of mint tea I picked up at the mercantile back there in Two-Penny. It smelled nice. Fellow said it's tasty and good for what ails you." I shrugged and sipped my own cupful of nothing but hot water. "I liked the smell."

I hated the taste of the lie in my mouth and hated even more that it had burst out of my mouth so readily.

He grunted and scrunched his eyes closed, moved his head back and forth slowly, as if he were trying to clear his mind but had no strength to do it. Then he forced his eyes open again and stared me down. "You . . . you tricked me. Lied to me, Roamer. How could you?"

I couldn't look at him. I looked down at the cup in my lap, ran my thumb over the rim.

"Damn you! I should be there!" He bellowed the words, the veins on his neck and the sides of his block head pulsing with fierce rage. His battered body would not let him do what he knew he needed to do, what his willful mind told him he must do. Finally, he sagged against the wadded blankets, shaking, spent. Even in the dim lantern light I saw the skin above his beard, his nose and cheeks and forehead, had turned papery and gray, a color I've only ever seen on dead men.

"You will be there." I leaned closer, my knuckles grinding into the sagged bedding. "Jack, it has to be this way. You're too ill. Trust me. Let me do this for you. You taught me all I know, made me all I am. You are as much a part of me as I am. Closer than a father, closer than a friend, closer than a brother. There is no word for what you are to me. You'll be there. And when I find Winter Woman, you'll know it." I leaned back on my haunches. "But I can't very well bring her back to someone who looks as bad as you do."

His filmy eyes slowly cut over to me. I prayed I'd hear it. *Say it, Jack.* I willed him to say it. I wanted to hear him call me an insolent pup. I don't think I could go on if he didn't show that spark, that arched-brow look that presages one of the many verbal and often physical tirades he finds so delicious. *Get up out of that bed and chase me with that tomahawk, old man. Come now, let's fight it out. Like old times. Call me an insolent pup. I promise this time I won't laugh and dodge your feisty blows.*

Instead, he closed his eyes and shook his head slowly and turned his face away from me, toward the wall.

If I had any doubt up to that moment, which I really hadn't, seeing him withered and broken like that told me I would go on alone. And the sooner I got to it, the better.

By the time I walked back to the fireplace, I heard Jack's breathing, slow and steady, in a deep sleep.

I wrote him a note that said about the same thing I'd told him a few moments before, in case he should forget. He'd find it once he discovered my treachery, for that's what it felt like to me. I hoped I could make this right, otherwise I was risking the truest friendship I'd ever had. Nonetheless, I had to do it. I finished the note and set a squat, empty green-glass bottle atop it on a low table beside the bed.

I laid more bedding over him, tucked in the edges, then piled more wood in the fireplace. He'd be out for some hours, given the tea and his run-down condition. I looked about the cabin once more, then blew out the lamp beside the bed, and set matches beside it.

Then I crossed the room and tugged the blanket off the gear I'd piled in the corner. I hefted the bundle and left. After tugging the door tight behind me, I wedged rags into the bottom gap from the outside, to stop the breeze.

I hoped the note would convince him to stay put and heal up. If he felt he had to follow, which he might well do, headstrong as Maple Jack was, at least I'd gained myself some time to get gone. That trail was beyond cold and by now more than unfollowable, but I had no choice. A wrong had been done and, for good or ill, I can't abide such. I must stick my sniffer in and make a wrong a right. And besides, I made a promise to Jack.

The wind still whipped, but had pinched to a pale version of its former blustering self. The sky had begun to lighten and I saw the winking of stars to the north, the direction from which the storm had come and the direction I needed to travel. The last of it would be gone within an hour, replaced with dawn's light.

I trudged through snow well above my knees, and kicked away enough of it to tug open the stable door. The warmth, mixed with the off-stink of dung and urine from Tiny and Mossy, pushed into my face. "Hello, boys," I said, blinking back stinging tears from the cold, then the warm and the stink. "Have you righted around in a minute."

I ran a hand along each beast's back and checked their feed and water. I'd filled everything before the storm and they'd not made much of a dent in either. Still, I topped it all up, two water buckets for each, and as much hay and feed as I could squirrel away into the racks and trough. Of course, they muzzled into the oats first thing.

"No sense hogging those down, there won't be more for a few days at least." They ignored me and kept eating. That's always the way. I sighed. "When I get back, we'll have to work on your English, okay? My horse and mule lingo isn't convincing enough, apparently."

Next, I shoved open the single door that led to the small corral. I squeezed through and kicked more snow away from it on the outside, then jerked the door enough so they could get in and out, if they did it without fighting to see who went first. They were old chums, so I doubted there would be much bother between them. Mossy was a quiet sort, but he'd show his teeth if Tiny Boy got too uppity. It would be good for Tiny to have a few days of humility.

With that last commitment taken care of, I said goodbye to the lads. I retrieved my snowshoes from the peg on the stable wall where I'd hung them when I unpacked the day before. I saw another pair, familiar to me, leaning in the corner. I'd missed seeing them earlier. I hefted them. They were Jack's.

I gave the other dark corners a quick scout but didn't see another pair. Maybe she didn't have any. I doubted this, but I didn't have more time to waste. I carried them outside with mine, leaned his against the stable, and strapped on mine. Then I pulled on my pack, not an easy task, especially with the Sharps strapped to the side, though I tried to pack light.

I topped that with the big buffalo hide coat I'd brought with me from Jack's cabin, knowing I'd need it in the high country. I left my wool mackinaw spread atop Jack. It'd be big on him, but I figured when he came to, he could use it to amble about the place. Or, if he was still steamed enough with me, he could always burn it. I half wondered if he might.

The buffalo coat is warmer than having a woodstove on your back. It's also heavy. I'd have laid it across Jack, but under all those other wool blankets and deerskins, he'd be more than warm. If I stood a chance in the high country, I'd need it. Even if it did weigh half of what I do.

Lastly, I readjusted my fur cap and lifted the big earflaps so they jutted outward. I'd tie them up atop my head later. I stomped in place a time or two, then grabbed Jack's snowshoes and hung them on a branch nub a good ten feet up in a tree. He'd see them, but it would take him a whole lot of work to get at them. As I trudged northward, I wondered if I was doing the right thing, leaving Jack behind alone, leaving Tiny and Mossy, hanging the snowshoes, all of it. A hundred-and-one evil possibilities flitted through my mind, clouding my previous conviction like moths on a lantern's globe on a warm, summer evening.

I didn't know if I was doing the right thing or not, but I was doing something, come what may. And that's exactly what Jack told me all those years before. "Boy, when you don't know what to do, go ahead and do something. Worse that can happen is you found out you did the wrong thing, then you know where you stand. So you go back and start over and do the right thing. Can't fail, see?"

"Yep, Jack," I said, as I stomped my way northward toward the dark brooding bulk of the mountain peaks looming so close before me. "Can't fail."

CHAPTER TWELVE

Even with the snowshoes, the going was difficult. I have mentioned I am not a small fellow, and with such a large frame and thick legs and big feet, why, there's only so much a person can ask of a pair of bentwood snowshoes, no matter how robust they are. That said, they made the going smoother than I had a right to. I would be foundering in the first drift a quarter mile from the cabin had I not been wearing them. Still, the trail was a challenge.

By the time the midday sun teased me with its fiery color, if not its too-distant warmth, I had traveled a number of miles and the peaks before me did what the mountains always do, no matter the range nor the state or territory or region I'm traveling through—they never drew any closer. It's one of those oddnesses in life we all must endure.

I'd long since passed the spot where I'd left off in my tracking from before the storm and was now traveling in a direction I could but guess at. At this elevation there were plenty of landmarks against which to set my course. I chose a distant boulder-top poking through the snow or a lone tree that I wouldn't mistake for another as I trudged, and then I made for it. So long as it wasn't a shadow or a cloud, I was doing well.

I once met a fellow who told me he'd gotten so far off-course, he ended up heading dead west instead of east, the direction he'd intended, and all because he followed a cloud he mistook for a snowy peak. By the time he figured out his mistake, he was so far along in his travels that he abandoned his plans to return to Pennsylvania and open a hardware store.

Instead, he found himself in Colorado, so he kept going. When I met him, he had married a woman who was working a fairly profitable gold claim left to her by her deceased husband, along with six children, a sour mood, and a hound with three legs. Better him than me.

So long as my chosen goal, be it tree or rock, was on the path I'd set for myself, this simple system worked. It also afforded me stretches of time while I was making for the next waypoint to think, something Jack says I do too much of. As with being homely and too big, it's not something I can help.

I'd hoped the trail left by the absconders would be simple enough to follow, but that was before the storm. I was left, now and again, with a slight depression that I took to be their trail. Either that or it was a game trail. I'd find out. I had to follow something, after all.

As I trudged, I scooped snow with my mittens and kept myself wet within and without, as Jack says when he swigs from his jug. He also says rainy days are drinking days. That way he keeps his innards as wet as his outside, lest he warp.

I had been correct—the snowfall as I ventured higher was significant. And from the vistas ahead, it wasn't about to become anything but thicker, deeper, and more challenging. No time for whining, Roamer, I told myself. After all, this is what I wanted. Not for the last time on this trip did I question my fanciful motivations.

It was during one of my scoopings of snow that I fell to ruminating about my big ol' mittens. They are the warmest pair I've ever had. A double thickness of tight-knitted, green wool. Even if they get wet, as with all garments made of wool, they retain heat and keep a body warm. They were made for me by a kindly old Quaker woman, a widow, in the south of Idaho Territory. I'd done a few days' worth of chores for her some time ago, perhaps a year or more, now that I think on it. Where does the time scurry off to?

She remains dear to me for many reasons, not the least of which are the mittens. She was unafraid of me from the start, and gave a genuine smile when I showed up and offered to split a jumble of stove-length rounds for her in exchange for a spot in her little barn for the night for me and Tiny. It had smelled like rain as I was passing the tidy place, so it seemed logical to seek out shelter rather than withstand a soaking. Tiny Boy's easier to live with if he's out of the elements in inclement weather.

Her husband, I came to learn over bowls of tasty soup and hunks of crusty, dark bread, had been a preacher of some sort, who she said preached kindness and gentleness in all doings.

"No matter the circumstance?" I said, gently testing the theory.

"No matter," she said, shaking her head and smiling. Actually, I don't believe that smile ever left her face.

That pile of split wood led to chicken coop repairs, and that led to reshingling two suspect spots on her shack's roof, and so on. Before I knew it, I'd spent a pleasant week encamped, along with Tiny Boy, in her small barn. I would have gladly stayed on and helped with anything else that needed doing, so pleasant was her company and her sincere kindness to me. In truth, it was like a balm I hadn't known I needed.

Finally, I knew one morning I had to move along once more. "Will you be all right here, ma'am?"

She laughed and patted my arm. She had to raise her arm to do this, she was that short. Yet she was anything but frail. She told me I reminded her of her late husband. Mortimer was his name. Hers was Abigail. She said she saw a kindness in me, the same as in him. I didn't offend her by claiming false modesty. I thanked her for the sincere compliment. It was, and remains, among the kindest things anyone has ever said to me.

Before Tiny Boy and I took our leave that morning, she gave me these mittens she'd knitted for me while I was out in her yard working her chores. She knitted the mittens from a sweater she'd made for her husband, his favorite sweater, she said, many, many years before, when—she blushed as she said it—they were "young lovers."

She also gave me a book that had belonged to her husband. I tried to refuse that, saying I couldn't possibly accept so much kindness from her. But she shook her head and her smile dipped for the first time.

I'll never forget what she said next: "I am old. You must not refuse me this. I will not live many more years, and then what will happen to it? It is of great importance that a book's journey never stops. It must continue to be shared, otherwise the author, the thinker, the mind, the person behind the words, the one who penned the words, will shine a little less with each season the book sits on a shelf unread. This is as much a crime as any. I have given away all the other books in the house as time has gone on, to people I felt were worthy and who could be trusted to share these words. Who I could be assured would share the words in turn once they had absorbed them. But this is the last and I have been waiting for the right person to come along. You are that person."

The book was *Walden; or Life in the Woods,* by one Henry D. Thoreau, and it altered much about me, my way of viewing the world, of living in this world, which for too long had seemed to me a harsh, cruel place filled with hard, grasping people bent on misdeeds and filled with bitterness and ill will. I was wrong.

There are foul people about us, to be sure, but they are a blight that, if the rest of the crop is strong, will soon be overtaken and subsumed, or stifled and choked out by the overwhelming goodness around them. I choose to believe this, anyway. I have to. Otherwise, I'll be what I was and that is not who I care to be any longer.

She taught me that simple lesson. Henry David Thoreau went on to teach me an untold number of other lessons, beginning with the importance of spending time out of doors and thinking. It had been reassuring to know I had, indeed, been on that path.

As I walked along on that mountainside, my breath clouds rising before my red face, I felt the reassuring weight of that volume in my coat's inner pocket. Its slight thickness and shape pressed against my side, small but good comfort on a journey I wasn't certain would lead me to anything good at all.

I hoped I'd find out soon. If not, I was carving a trail to nowhere, deeper and deeper into the mountains where men did not venture in the cold and snowy months. Would I find blight or the inevitable end of a fool's folly?

CHAPTER THIRTEEN

The night, or at least the darkness, came soon, as it does at this time of year. Sooner than I wanted it to. It never fails, even on frigid days, I will push and tell myself, "Five minutes more," then I'll be five minutes closer to wherever it is I will find myself tomorrow. Trouble is, my five minutes always end up lasting twenty.

The air had cooled with the quick slump of the sun behind the jutting Bitterroot Range to my left, the west. This caught me short and reminded me of my foolishness to wring out the juice from the day.

Even though I knew I would set up camp in the coming dark, when day's light withers and leaves me in blue-purple gloom, I couldn't help myself. Despite my mission, I was in a place I love, winter in the mountains. This was not how I expected or intended to enjoy this place and time, but while I made my way deeper in, I vowed to see everything I could, to take it all in.

When I did stop, it was at a perfect spot, backed against a solid berm of drift. Sculpted like sandstone and packed by wind and the day's sun, it needed little shaping by me. I would do what I could anyway. But before that, I needed a fire. And before *that,* I needed to shuck off those snowshoes. I did, standing them upright and close at hand.

Now, to attend to the fire. My flint and steel and ball of woolly duff would serve to kindle flame, but first I needed tinder and then larger branches to feed those flames. A quick trip into the surrounding pines with my hip knife furnished me with a raft of dead branches. I skinned off softer, greener boughs here and there for sleeping.

I try never to take more than a tree feels as though it wants to give up. Fanciful thinking on my part, I know, for if I were a tree, I doubt I would want some big goober hacking off any of my limbs for his fire and comfort. Likely not, but at the end of the silent argument and pinch of guilt I always feel when limbing a tree, I am the one with the knife, the one with a need for comfort and warmth. *Besides,* I reasoned with a wry grin, *I bet I could outrun a tree.*

Four strikes in, and sparks danced in the balled duff into which I struck the steel and flint. I huffed gentle but insistent breaths at it and then, and this always surprises and delights me, fire bloomed to life.

What magical conjuring I am able to get up to, day after day, dusk after dusk, to welcome this dormant friend back to my camp, to visit with me a while. All he asks is that I feed him. I suspect Jack feels the same about me when I show up. The difference between me and flame is that I tend to eat more on my visits.

I saw no need for a full snow cave that night, as it was clear and still. Once the fire had been suitably welcomed and fed its first course of vittles, I scooped into the snow, toward the hillside, the bulk of the mountains to my back. The deepest part of the hollow, I would use for sleeping.

I arranged the green boughs for my bed, which sounds fancier than it is. I laid them this way and that until they got me up off the snow and cushioned my bulk. That wouldn't last, I knew from past experience, but it would be enough to nudge me into sleep.

I freed the Sharps and stood it close by. Then I dragged out the items I needed from my pack—my small tin pot for melting snow and making coffee, a handful of hardtack crackers, and three lengths of jerky. I'd rummage later for an apple. I set the pot by the edge of the fire to begin making water from snow. The food bits, I stuffed in my coat pockets.

I've unintentionally shared more than one bite of food with mice and squirrels, and didn't feel like making their acquaintance on this night, no thank you. I fetched wood, punching into the same holes I'd made before and coming back with enough to keep my small fire lively company for some hours. Then I made one more trip for good measure.

I was some hungry, and I knew I still would be after I ate, but I hadn't wanted to kill anything for broiling over my fire tonight. Somehow, with all the brutish treatment and Jack's bloodied head, and his and Winter Woman's forced-apart lives so fresh in my mind, I didn't feel like splashing more blood and cracking the silent mountain air with the sudden sound of a gunshot. I would hunt tomorrow if I needed to. But not today.

I spent those early evening hours in quiet, the darkness closing off sight of the vast, slow slope before me, the peaks to my back, the trees, blacker with each passing minute, stippling the night on all sides. Soft scuffs of snow sounded upslope to my right, southwestward. What would be out in the mountains in the snow in the dark? A wolverine?

Could be anything, but random and soft enough and without accompanying panting breaths that would hint it was not human, and for that I was thankful. The scuffing stopped, and I listened for long minutes after the last sound came to me.

A breeze traveling southward alone soughed high up in the pines, a whisper, then went on its way. A thought came to me then that a breeze, wind, gust, gale, what have you, cannot stay in one place. It must always move. Or it will die. No, perhaps that's not correct. It will cease to be.

I wonder if people are like that, or perhaps should be. I know if I spend too long in any one place, I fidget and worry and find myself unable to pay attention to the things at hand that I should. Yet when I travel with Tiny Boy, or alone, as I was then, I am content, as a breeze must be, ever moving.

Well, I was nearly content. And no doubt would be, were it not for the beasts that snatched Winter Woman from her life. Thoughts of those dark creatures, whom Jack was convinced were blood-eyed, murderous devils, pushed aside any hope I'd had of reading even a page or two from Thoreau's fine book.

I've read it enough that I could spout its intent and even parrot passages, front to back, so I should not be as disappointed as I was, and yet I sighed low and long. Time to give over to puzzling out the predicament once more—the very conundrum I'd spent much of the day's journey considering.

The basic situation was thus: Jack and Winter Woman had been attacked. The assailants hadn't wanted Jack, or even wanted him dead, just subdued. They also had not wanted much of anything of value that Winter Woman may have had. But they did want her. Did they snatch her because she was a woman? That notion led to dark, grim thoughts.

Or did they snatch her because she was a healer? I hoped that was the situation. If so, why not ask for her help? Why resort to violence? Perhaps she refused them? Not likely. According to Jack, she was forever interrupting her own daily pursuits to gather tinctures and herbs and help someone in need. So, I asked myself again, why the violence?

And who were they, these two-legged, barefooted, devilish creatures who possibly needed the help of a healer? Oddly, I hoped I would soon find out. Imagine that, me wishing for trouble.

It was sometime in the dark belly of night that I awoke, bundled tight and stiff with cold. The one bit of skin exposed to the frigid, still air was my nose tip. I'd swaddled my head with a scarf wrapped tight over my big fur hat, the earflaps tugged down and tied beneath my chin. On my hands I wore a spare pair of wool socks over my mittens.

If there's any bit of kit I carry extra of, year-round, it's socks. I'm forever wearing out the heels, then darning them. But I don't mind. They keep my feet and hands warm, and that counts for a whole lot when I'm hunkered in a snowdrift. But it wasn't the cold that woke me that night. It was the wolves.

At least I thought it was wolves. I heard feet padding through snow, intermittent sounds of crunching, as if one was hopping from spot to spot. What made me think *wolves* were the irregular huffing, snuffling, snorting sounds that drifted down to me in my hidey-hole in the snow. How were they staying up on the snow's surface? Ah, they weren't, that's what made for the hopping, irregular crunches. They were leaping through it. And from the sounds of their ragged breaths, there were many of them. And they were drawing closer.

I have long heard street-corner stories, spoken in low tones, of people on remote farms, trappers caught between line shacks, cowboys lost in blizzards, and others, children, women, the old, all savaged, so the husky-voiced gossips have said, by ravenous wolves in winter. I have heard the stories, and I have for the most part dismissed them. I've seen plenty of wolves over the years. Months earlier found me watching with my spyglass a pack of timber wolves in high summer, lolling in the sun, the youngsters feeling frisky, then twitching with tension and stalking with elaborate care before pouncing on their parents' heads. They reminded me of human families I've seen on the trail, wagon-rolling emigrants resting on a Sunday, the father smoking a pipe, the mother napping beneath her flop-brim bonnet, the children squealing and chasing each other before collapsing on their parents' legs in mock exhaustion. No, I had little faith in the stories of wolves as savage killers.

Then why on this frigid night, with a slivered moon and more stars than there are snowflakes in the mountains, were these wolves prowling close by? Was I merely trespassing on their home range? Were they nothing more than curious about this big galoot with the weird smells? How well could they see in the night? And would they think me, wrapped in my buffalo robe coat, some wayward, toothsome treat?

This was but an early blizzard of what would be a long winter season. Were they unprepared and hungry? Though I didn't give much credence to the stories I'd heard, I was becoming worried. So I did what I always do when I come up against something of which I'm uncertain—I faced it with what strengths I had.

They were close, so I had little time. I sat up, got to my knees, used my teeth to tug off my left mitten and sock, then removed those on the right. I unbuttoned the big antler toggles holding my coat closed, and spread it wide. The cold air rushing into my clothing tent pierced me, refreshed me, and snapped my eyes wider than wide.

I considered the Sharps but decided against it for now. I'd keep it at hand, but a single-shot rifle is too heavy and awkward and slow for close-in work. I pulled out my Schofield, checked it was loaded, then laid my hand on the handle of my big hip knife. I heard the padding from up above, how far away, I don't know. Perhaps a dozen feet, maybe more.

The fire, I thought, *I should revive the fire.* Its coals still glowed little more than an arm's length before me. I leaned forward and laid on more duff, then twigs and snapped branches from the small pile I'd prepared for a morning coffee flame. I blew on the coals and stopped, listened. More sounds. Then they, too, stopped.

Were they watching me? I blew on the coals and was rewarded with tiny, licking flames. I added more tinder, then bigger sticks.

Smoke swirled up. Surely they smelled it, surely it would bother them, back them up. Surely.

And yet, as the flames bloomed taller, wider, I fancied I saw shadows twenty feet out, well beyond my meager fire's growing glow. I added more wood, knowing I would run out before long.

Then the shadows moved and the stars blinked. Yellow stars. Far too close to the ground. They were no stars, they were eyes.

CHAPTER FOURTEEN

As I said earlier, the last time I faced down a pack of winter-starved timber wolves was . . . never. So to wake up hearing panting and snuffling and low snarls circling, drawing closer, not twenty feet from my paltry campsite, was a tip-off that all was not well in my little frozen hunk of winter wilderness.

Despite sucking in lungfuls of the frigid air, I was somewhat sleep dazed, blinking and trying to figure out my best next move. I had a feeling I wouldn't have long to indulge in my figuring. The moon's weak, blue glow on this cloudless night was enough to offer me a glimpse of a dark shape. That's when the first wolf lunged.

The hairy brute grew larger the closer it flew at me. Its mouth opened and its jaws stretched wide and tall, revealing yellow fangs that flickered wet and drippy with spittle in reflected firelight.

I'd say it was a good three feet from me when something slammed into me from my left side, shoving me to the snow and knocking my revolver from my hand. Where the gun landed, I knew not. From the force of the blow, I guessed it spun away off to my right, into the darkness. At that moment, I didn't have time to consider it. For the beast that had slammed into me had also lost its footing, but was not as quick as I in righting itself.

In that eyeblink of time when the side-lunging wolf rammed me, the first wolf, which had been robbed of its head-on prize, disappeared from my sight. I shoved back upright to my knees and did not know the first wolf had piled up behind me.

This irked it even more, and it came at me snapping and snarling, those fantastic jaws slavering wide and taking in a mouthful of my thick fur-hide coat. I had so many layers draped on my big body that there was little danger the wolf would break through any time soon.

I had to deal with the side jumper, who'd regained control of himself and started in on my right side. He collided again with me as I shoved back up to my knees.

The stink of the beasts, the raw, hairy, mauling, kill-driven sweat of them, cut through the bone-snapping cold of the night and startled me like a kick to the jaw. My nostrils rebelled and my throat gagged. My raging mind was the one thing about me that took offense enough to stay with the fight. It commanded my big, meaty fists, which, now shed of their warming mitten cocoons, grabbed at the attacker.

I swung my right arm around, hoping to slam it with a wild blow, but its own big jaws clamped on that outstretched arm. All I felt was a slight pressure, but I sure saw those eyes and that big glistening black nose. All taking me in, the nose twitching like a living thing all its own, snuffling and perched above that wide-stretched mouth that kept on gnawing and shaking back and forth.

I'm not a small boy, but between that wolf hanging off the back of me and the wolf ripping at me from the side, each one of them jerking on me like I was a rope two teams of schoolchildren were playing tug-across with, I could hardly keep upright. The reason I did, I imagine, is because their separate efforts balanced each other out. I waited on no one, never do in a fight, and I snatched at my hip knife with my left hand.

Problem was, the knife hangs on my right side, so I had to reach across my gut. I slid my hand beneath that big, flapping coat and felt the antler handle's reassuring, polished girth. I fumbled fast to wrap my fingers around it.

I could not take a chance at losing it to another slam. I didn't know how many more wolves were fixing to land on me from who knows what direction, so I had to keep that knife in hand. It was the one weapon I had left on me, save for my fists and mouth, which I have used in fights when it comes right down to it. A man who won't kick and bite and scratch and claw and scream his way out of a death-fight is no man, but a simpering, mewling creature who has given up on himself and, what's worse, on the most valuable thing we each of us have—our lives.

I did not give up. I fought like a demon.

I swung that big, heavy knife, honed to a shaving edge, like a guillotine down on that side-lunger's snout. Would have gone deeper, but my layers of coats and clothing limited my reach. It didn't matter, as my cut worked. It nearly severed that bastard's muzzle.

He tried to scream, but his sounds were quickly drowned by gushing blood. The noises that bubbled up from his throat were a bloodied blend of gagging and clotted, wet howl.

The top jaw, still attached to the bottom by strings of gristle and hair and jutting bone shards, was also still attached to my sleeve, as the fangs had sunk into the hide of the coat. The beast, in its thrashing agony, tore itself from that top jaw, leaving snout and snot-strings of blood and all swinging from my arm.

As for the rest of the wolf, though it had been a killing, demonic-looking thing before it became a bloodied mess, it whipped away from me, snapping itself side to side, gouting blood up out of its hideous, gaping maw.

I could no longer see its eyes, so filmed were they with its own gore. It staggered and writhed backward to the ring of light thrown by my still-flickering campfire. That's when I saw at least another dozen sets of eyes in shadow, roving, blinking, narrowed in rage. Then they all lunged for the roiling, bloodied beast in their midst. The sounds were hideous and brutal as the beasts savaged each other in their clawing efforts to get to the dying, thrashing wolf.

I stood, the wolf behind me still swinging and jamming its forepaws into me for traction. It hung from me, bucking and clawing, and found new purchase as if I were a mountain of fur, flesh, and blood to scale and then consume. It would summit to my skull soon.

I thrashed back and tried to swing it side to side to dislodge it, all the while grabbing at it with my right hand while my left still held the big knife in a firm grip. I managed to muckle onto a leg and the beast tensed even more but did not let go its fang-hold between my shoulders. I lurched backward, half staggering, and went down on my right side, plunging into the snow with the wolf atop me.

The fall gave it an excuse to let go of its bite and readjust. It sought my head, specifically the parting space between my coat's big collar and my fur hat. My neck was exposed then, for I felt its hot breath closing in on me.

I jerked its leg hard and felt something give. The beast, for all its brute tactics, whined high and loud, right in my ear. A shriek like a kicked puppy will make. Good, I thought. For though I detest violence, and certainly that inflicted on animals (human and otherwise), all cards are on the table when I'm under attack.

I reached around with my left arm and tried to rip the wolf off my back, but it shot over my right shoulder, its long, coarse animal hide grazing my face. Then it scampered straight into the boiling frenzy of wolves a dozen feet from me.

I shoved back to my feet and stood, spraddle-legged, my breathing coming in ragged gasps, the slick-bladed knife poised before my chest, my right arm held up as if it wore a medieval shield. I was as ready as I could be for a next attack. And I knew without doubt it would happen, and soon.

They would tire of eating one of their own and come at me once more. I was a prize they sought. The unfortunate wolf had merely been a toothsome distraction. I was big, pink, and fleshy, or so I assumed that was how they regarded me. A lumbering beast covered in fur that could be taken down by their renewed, multiple-angle attacks of cunning.

I waited, not taking my eyes from them, half-conscious of my breathing and trying to slow it, steady it, level it off. I would need my wind for a nightlong battle. I tried to count their number and was stymied with every whipping, thrashing lunge the wolves made.

Even the one whose leg I broke was in there somewhere, not caring that I'd dealt what surely in the coming weeks could be a death blow. What good is a three-legged wolf in hunting prey? Perhaps I was wrong. Perhaps they were so willful, this pack, that they'd ignore such a wound.

For some time, they went at the now-dead wolf, the one whose face I had lopped off. I looked down at my arm, reminded of the vile thing, and still the top half of the ragged snout hung from my sleeve. I snatched it with my left hand and threw it into the midst of the roiling mass of wolves. It disappeared among them.

I checked for the carbine and found it close by, right where I'd leaned it. I pulled it closer and waited.

And so went the long night.

CHAPTER FIFTEEN

Dawn came slow that day, slower than it has ever come in my life. They say a watched pot fails to boil. The same with a morning sky. It will not show itself while you watch for it. But I watched, having lost patience, along with so much else, over the course of the vicious night that seemed more like a brutal, unending death dream than something I lived through.

I've seen wolves many times throughout my slow travels. But none like these. Not only were they twice the size of any I've ever seen, but they acted strange, stranger than any of those others.

Why had they attacked? The two I'd had close contact with didn't appear to be starved. Their coats were, if not sleek, at least thick and bore a distinct luster. But the odd thing, even in the low light, was that they were all dark-colored, some of them nearly black. Their yellow eyes and yellow-white fangs the lightest things of color about them.

All this and more I pondered as I waited for daylight to raise its slow, lazy head.

And when it did, I was rewarded with a scene I will not long forget. What had been a pristine white landscape all about me when I settled into my modest campsite at dusk the day before now resembled the fresh filth of an abattoir.

Spattered gore had leached into the snow all about my camp in a ragged half circle. Matted into it were tufts of gray-black hair, lighter at the base, along with splinters of snapped bone, crushed, no doubt, by the brutal, slashing jaws of those big wolves. They hadn't looked starved, so I can guess they had boiled themselves into a frenzy of killing lust, turning on their fellow wolves with what appeared to be glee.

Their tracks formed a trampled, bloodied scene that spiraled outward, with my wee camp as the nexus. The more I gazed in shock at the churned, red-black scene before me, the more I saw, including my snowshoes, no longer jammed upright in the snow but dragged in opposite directions. The webbing on one had been gnawed through, and the other had sustained damage to the wide, curved edge.

They still appeared to be useful, so that was one less worry. As to others, I needed to find my Schofield. The last I'd seen it, or rather felt it, was when it had sailed, spinning into the night, from my grasp when the wolf slammed into me. I walked back to the spot I'd fought from, hefted the rifle, and mimicked my stance during the fight.

I rummaged for several minutes through fur chunks, bloody snow, and bone shards. In my search, I toed up several churned-in lengths of hairy wolf scat, thinking the dark coloring might be the gun's walnut grips. I finally nudged the now-frozen gun revolver with my boot. I lifted it and noticed with a grunt of satisfaction that it appeared whole, though frozen and wet.

I laid it on my blankets at the spot I'd fought from and returned to the wider area about me. The snowshoes and the gun would prove the simplest of my items to retrieve. Somehow the woods-dogs had managed to make off with my pack. I had no idea how they got up to such boldness, especially not while it was so close by me the entire time. That very thought chilled me. Right beside me.

Somehow one of the sneaky beasts had padded up that close to me, within a foot or two, while I had stood, trembling, gripping my knife, mesmerized by the boiling tumult before me, and awaiting a second attack.

Had I really been that blinded, that distracted, by them? The backpack was not small, either, but a canvas affair with leather straps and brass buckles, and though I'd packed as light as possible, it was still laden with food, a pan, my small coffee pot, spare socks, extra bullets, and a few other items. Turns out it was easy to track, as the sneaky beast that had nabbed it had left a drag trail that led a good two hundred feet off into the trees. It must have been hard going, walking backward and tugging on that cumbersome sack, all the while keeping an eye out for me and for his or her packmates.

Still, that was odd behavior, I thought, as I stood looking down at the pack in the snow and glaring into the trees. With unpredictable critters such as those wolves, it would do no good to assume they were afraid of sniffing me out again.

As I bent to the pack, a pungent stink like meat gone off in full sun rolled off the sack in waves, pulsing, it felt, right at my face and into my nostrils.

It was horrible.

Then I saw a wad of discolored snow and knew the wolf had urinated on my backpack. I moaned and tweezered shut my nostrils with one hand while lifting the pack up off the snow with a hooked finger on my other. That would be too ripe to wear.

The pack, I saw as I raised it, had been gnawed on. One of the straps was nearly chewed through, and the critter had managed to nibble a finger-size hole in the bottom, but that was all. Something must have scared it off. I was grateful to whatever had done so, though I wish it could have done it before the thing peed on my goods.

I trudged back to the campsite and took in the rest of the carnage. My meager woodpile, which I had been counting on to make coffee, had been knocked over in the melee, and that, too, had been urinated all over. There were numerous knots of scat throughout the gory scene, too.

It was as if they weren't merely trying to kill me, they also wanted me to know I was trespassing on their domain. For that's what I had become convinced was the situation. They were warning me off. If that attack had been merely a shot across my bow, I had better put thought into what a second round would do.

I sighed. "Good morning, Roamer," I said as I bent to begin the task of tidying and cleaning what little of use was left to me.

As soon as I made my piles, I washed in snow, stripped to the waist, and scrubbed myself until pink. If the bastards decided to attack right then, I'd be sunk.

CHAPTER SIXTEEN

After I'd cleaned myself and the gear to the best of my abilities, mending what required it, I heated snow using the least offensive lengths of the urine-soaked wood left to me, and then bundled up all and sundry and set off on my trek northward into the dark, brooding mountains looming above me.

Though the day promised to be a good one, with blue skies and the barest of light clouds breaking up far away, a marrow-deep feeling of foreboding soured my mood. Well, that and the fact that I was now traveling in a cloud of stink the wolves thought fit to leave me with.

It made my eyes water. Heck, who am I kidding? It made me want to shout at anything I saw move. And I did, too, including a rabbit and a hawk. After a few miles, I mellowed and even tried to whistle when I saw a grouse darting back under low-swept pines after I swung his way.

It was while I was in the middle of a long, wide shelf of snow, pristine and untouched by any creature, save for a bird shadow that slid across its whiteness, that I first felt the hairs on the back of my neck bristle up. It's a sensation I'm familiar with. It's the most useful form of instinct I know. Maple Jack calls it "listening to your gut." But since mine is nearly always hungry, I hear enough of it already. I'll stick with instinct. It works for every other critter on the earth, why not humans?

I paused, then resumed my walk, my arms swinging in great arcs fore and aft of me, and I angled my head the barest bit to

enable me to see downslope. I saw nothing but blinding whiteness and a slope stippled with trees and curved with wind-
carved drifts. Some with great swooping shelves jutting twenty
feet into the air, defying everything ever surmised about science. Beautiful, and if it hadn't been for that warning feeling, I
should have liked to enjoy the scene further.

But though I saw nothing far below, nor upslope, nor behind,
nor ahead, I knew I was being seen, being watched. But by
what? Or whom? I considered this as I walked on. Likely it was
the wolves tracking me. I made my way, huffing and sweating,
as the bright midday sun reflected off the vast snowfield.

At times the only things I saw that weren't draped in snow
were the craggy peaks all about me, the stunning blue sky above
it all, and, when I squinted ahead, further into the dark valley
beckoning above and before me, I saw dark spines of pines that
looked to be losing their needles the deeper into this dank
declivity I traveled. Soon, I expected, they would be nothing but
brittle, standing husks.

I swiveled my torso and looked behind me. Downslope, I
could have sworn I saw something slipping out of my sight line.
Wolves? I don't think so. Then what? What else could be secretive? Sneaky, even? Lurking coyotes, possibly. A man? It could
not be Jack, for he was so stoved up and addled when I left him
that though I believed he would make do for himself in the
cabin, I don't think he would last long on the trail. Even given
that the man has never failed to surprise me with his grit and
determination, this time, I feared he was not up to the task.

With that cheerful thought, and little else in my mind, I
doubled my huffing efforts and trudged onward.

The day was a bright blue one, as I have mentioned, but the
trail I followed led me toward a high-up gorge that, despite the
full sun of the day, appeared shrouded in a thick, low gauze of
gray cloud, like fog that hugs coastal waters. What lay in there,

ahead and higher up, deeper into the crotch of these mountains, I knew not. Were I prone to fanciful notions and had I an impressionable mind, they might lend more reason for concern about my vague chill of foreboding. Had I been a barefoot brute who stole people from their lakeside cabins, I could hardly choose a more ideal hidey-hole. The reasons why someone would act so would have to wait.

I say it is a trail I followed, but really it was a guess at a trail. The storm covered any true pathway and tracks and left me to speculate. But again, it was a guess based on instinct. And the knowledge that should I not choose a direction, I would get nowhere at all. Any direction is a leg up on that.

It was hours later, close to the time I began snooping for a campsite protected from attack on at least one side, that I felt the sensation once more. This time I was quite certain I was being watched. Once, twice more I spun with as much surprise as I could muster, but I saw nothing.

I trudged on, more convinced than ever, but for now there was nothing I could do about it. Though I was not certain of my direction, I knew that traveling deeper into the mountains, somehow, was the answer. I decided to venture further into the darkness ahead, despite the bright freshness of the snowpack.

Ahead I saw trees thickening, a welcome sight as it meant protection from the wind that had begun whipping up, protection of some sort from the beasts still on my backtrail. It also meant fuel for a fire. I could use hot food and coffee. I was thankful once more that the wolf did not make off with my supplies. Something fortuitous warned it away before it could deal proper damage.

Grateful to have my pack, I wished that rude critter hadn't peed all over it. I scoured it with snow and ice chunks, but the onion-soaked-in-old-socks stink never left me all day. Nor, I suspected, would it tomorrow.

That was all the thought I had time for. I heard a loud, deep thud, like far-off cannon fire, but close enough to bring me to a stop. I stood and listened. The sound did not repeat itself. But it did have an effect. With no warning, the mountainside above me let go its precious claw hold on the craggy heights. A massive wave of snow, as if it were the mountainside itself, slid straight at me.

Instinct snagged me once more and I ran forward as if I'd had a full night's sleep and a hearty, strengthening meal— neither of which I had within me. Even with seconds to live I knew my chance at survival lay ahead, beyond the oncoming flank of the great wall of snow from above. To run downslope meant a guarantee of death. Here I might cheat it with a pinch of all the luck accumulated and unused by all the persons and creatures in all the world.

A long shot, sure, but isn't that why we're here? To play the odds, to buck the tiger, to bet the house, to risk the farm, to dare, every single day of our short, frightened lives? You bet it is. At least that's what I told myself as I ran like the hounds of hell themselves were sinking fangs into my backside.

CHAPTER SEVENTEEN

It didn't work.

I heard the sound of a hundred-hundred loaded freight wagons churned in a high-plains twister raking up everything in its path. I didn't dare look upslope to my left, because I feared if I saw what I knew was bearing down on me, I would simply halt. I'd stagger to a stop and stare at the biggest moving thing I'd ever seen as it pummeled me. Then I did look.

And a runaway locomotive on a downhill grade slammed into my left side. It shoved me as you might expect a train will do and kept on shoving.

Oddly enough, it wasn't my first avalanche. I kept thinking that as I was squeezed and pounded and clubbed and pierced and nearly torn limb from limb.

Some time ago, I was buried in a snowslide that had felt mammoth. It was by luck, and an angry wolverine, that I found my way to the surface, and so to life, once again. As I tumbled this time, I thought I might not be so lucky. Over and over, in the midst of the ruckus, the floor and the ceiling, the ground and the sky, I never knew which, fell away. Then everything went black, including my mind.

When I came to, as was my custom, I lay still and tried to get my bearings, physical and mental. Drip by drip, what had happened slowly came back to me. When the great wall of snow appeared in my mind, I screamed. And I screamed and screamed a bit more. After a string of such shenanigans, I shut up, because it occurred to me that I was able to scream, and I could hear myself screaming. And if that were the case, surely I was still alive.

Because if you're dead, you don't feel anything. Or so I suspect. Hmm. Shortly after all that screaming, I began to feel sore. My entire body was a pounded, thin-skinned side of beef.

I knew from my previous encounter with an avalanche that if you're buried alive in snow, it packs so tight about you, in you, in every place it can get into—pockets, mouth, hair, ears, eyes, nostrils, sleeves, socks—and yet I felt my arms lift, my hands touch my face. I felt my legs, sore as they were, bend at the knee. My neck, also mighty sore, moved my head side to side.

So I wasn't packed tight in snow. Then where was I? I groped in the dark, figured out I was laid out on my back. With much grunting and groaning, I rolled over on my side, then onto my stomach. My head, wobbly on my straining neck, clunked onto the floor. And it was a floor, or the ground. I tasted dirt on the tip of my tongue, cold, but not snow. Definitely dirt.

This made no sense. I was certain I hadn't imagined the snowslide. Maybe it had shoved me all the way down the mountainside to . . . where? And why was there no snow above me? I rolled partially over and tried to focus my eyes, to see if there were stars. Given the day we'd had, I imagined it would be a clear, starry night. And yet I saw no stars above me.

I raised an arm and reached forward, yet I felt nothing in the blackness. My fingers closed on nothing but themselves, on my palm. That meant I'd lost my mitten. Checked the other hand and yep, that mitten was gone, too.

Something else came to me then, as I patted my face—the second finger on my right hand felt bad. It was bent and likely broken. It hurt about as bad as a broken finger will hurt. I touched it gingerly with my left hand. It was swollen, the whole length of it. Likely purple, too.

With more effort and a whole lot of embarrassing gasps and moans, I inched forward on my knees with my hands stretched out before me. Within a foot or two I felt rock and dirt, firm soil. I recoiled at the first touch, then felt it again, palming it, then using it to lean against as I stood.

My knees made popping sounds like dry sticks in a fire, but other than those and my own heavy exhalations, I heard no sound. It was cold wherever I was, but it was not frigid, certainly not as cold as it had been the night before.

I also discovered I had lost my big fur hat and my backpack somewhere on my rough journey. That made me think of my snowshoes and I bent to grope at my boots. My left boot was free of anything resembling a snowshoe, and my right wore a couple of leather wraps, all that was left of the strapping that bound my boot to the snowshoe. As for the snowshoes themselves, I felt no sign of the curved-wood-and-rawhide affairs.

"Okay," I said, my voice sounding odd in the still blackness of wherever I was. "Where am I?" No echo. Dead, close air. Not stuffy, but cold and still. "Anybody else here?"

My voice cracked, my throat felt raw. Probably from all that screaming. That was odd, considering I'm not much for overt shows of emotion. But recalling the chilling sight that was about to end my life coming down on me was reason enough to yelp.

I paused a moment. Maybe that meant I really was dead? If that was the case, how come I felt so awful? I always figured when you were dead, there would be a whole lot of nothing, no awareness at all, certainly no pain. Yet here I was, sore all over and no doubt bruised and cut and battered. Nah, I couldn't be dead. If I was really going to indulge in fantasy thoughts, I should skip all the paltry things such as pain and soreness.

I smiled, despite my predicament. I was alive. That was something, anyway.

CHAPTER EIGHTEEN

I roved the spot I found myself in and discovered it was a pit, almost like a hand-dug well or an abandoned mine shaft. How high up it went, I had no idea, it was that dark. But I walked round and round, feeling up and down from as high as I could reach, down to where my boot toes clunked the sides.

I'd say it was six, seven feet across, maybe bigger at the bottom, and it widened, flaring outward, as it went up. I'm north of six feet tall and my hands can reach eight, nine feet up, but I felt more of the same, rocks and earth and tree roots. Or else they were frozen snakes. I hoped not. As near as I could tell, I was indeed in a pit, likely man-made for it to be so regular feeling. Beneath my feet, too, was telling, as it was fairly flat. Rarely in nature will you find much of anything that a human would call regular or normal.

As to the floor, it was hard-packed stone and earth, much like the walls, and free of debris. I prized a fist-size rock from the wall, then backed up as far as I could and lobbed the rock upward. I wanted to see how high up the ceiling was. I tossed it the once, holding my hands up to cover my head, out of instinct, I guess. I didn't hear the rock hit anything. Nor did I hear it fall back down. Maybe my hearing had been damaged.

As it was dark, I had to crawl around to find the rock again. That's when it occurred to me that I could try to light up the weird space. I rummaged in my coat and found my flint and steel. I also had a dozen or so matches, but I didn't want to use those until I had to. No telling how long I'd be here. I refused to let my mind go down the forever trail. No, that's not quite true, I did my best to prevent myself from thinking I might be in that hole forever.

My rock throwing experiment temporarily forgotten, I gathered up what I thought might burn, and found it wasn't much. I remembered my paltry bit of saved duff and fluff squirreled down into the bottom of my flint and steel sack, a small rawhide bag with a drawstring top that Jack made me some years ago. I had intended to top up my supply of woolly hairs and delicate curls of dry aspen bark. I could always slice off some of the hair from my coat. My concern was not in making a fire, but if I did, where would the smoke go?

For now, I reasoned, it would be wiser to take further stock of as much of my hole as I could, and then make decisions. What else did I have to burn, anyway? Not much, as it turned out. My palm briefly smacked the copy of *Walden*, still riding snugged in my pocket. No way was I going to tear up that book—or any book. At least not until I grew desperate. And even then, I'd have to give the notion a whole lot more thought.

Along about the time I was rooting in my pockets, taking care not to bump my broken finger—why is it that the more you try not to do something, the more you think about it and so the more you do that thing?—I thought of other possessions I might still have, namely my Schofield and my knife. My pack, along with all the gear and food inside, and my rifle on the outside, were gone, stripped from me.

Of the revolver, there was an empty holster. This trip had been hell on my poor gun. Part of me didn't care, as it was a tool I was not fond of, not because it will kill what it's aimed at, but because it's so blamed loud. I much prefer quiet implements, such as my knife, though a knife is hardly practical when you're hunting long distances or when you are braced by someone with a gun. It pays in such situations to have a gun of your own to brace them back with.

As to the knife, the unbroken fingers of my right hand closed with relief around the polished horn of the handle. I sighed out loud, and half expected someone to say, "What's wrong now?" But no, it was silent in my hole in the ground. Dead silent.

At least I assumed it was a hole in the ground. Where else would it be?

Finally, I cuffed the steel on flint and lit the duff and blew on it there on the floor before me. I added what other burnable bits I found in my coat pockets and scrounged from the floor. The light given was enough to glow up a ball of orange brightness in that gloomy hole. I gently lifted it aloft on the broad blade of my knife and held it up, hoping it would not snuff out before I was able to see something of my surroundings.

I was rewarded with a continued glow for less than a minute's worth of exploring. My fingertips had not lied, it was a hole, man-made, gouged out of the earth, and with no tunnels that I could see of any size radiating out from it.

Before the light pinched out, I held it up as high as I could without losing it off the knife blade. I couldn't be certain, but thought there might be whiteness up there. Did that mean snow? I stared upward, moving my head back and forth, trying to see what I could see. If that was snow up there, I could be in a world of hurt should it all cave in on me. Then the light snuffed out.

I stood wondering what to do and resolved that there wasn't much I could do should the snow drop on me. I sat down against the wall and sighed. Cold had begun to creep into my bones and I did my best to huddle deeper into my coat.

My bare head was hardly warmed by my shaggy topknot, but I raised up my collar and shoved my hands into my coat and brought my knees up close and did my best to consider my situation from all angles.

Mostly I was tired and as sore as a hammer-struck thumb. After a while, that's what got me. I slipped into sleep thinking of snow, snow, and holes in the ground, and snow. And as fretful as my bout of sleep was, what came next was worse.

CHAPTER NINETEEN

I heard a noise, a voice, maybe, but distant, muffled, as if someone were shouting through water. It kept on and I opened my eyes. I didn't notice at first that I could see, well, that I could see better than I'd been able to before I fell asleep. Then it came to me—I could see.

There were walls, shadowy and gaunt, instead of blackness all about me. I pulled up my hands and held them before my face. They were my hands, to be sure. Big and homely, and that second finger on the right was most definitely broken. The cold of the place made it throb.

With that thought, my teeth rattled. I stretched my neck and looked up and saw why I could now discern shapes. The roof glowed, faintly, a blue-gray, but it was there nonetheless. No wonder I couldn't touch it. I wagered it was seventeen, maybe twenty feet up. But why would it glow? Then it came to me. It was snow and it could not be all that thick, since it must be daylight shining through, forcing that cold glow down on me.

As I grunted and shoved to my feet, I heard the sounds I'd all but forgotten in my previous moments of wakeful wonder. They were most definitely shouts, and of the human sort. I could not make out the words, but I did not much care at that point. "Hey! Hey up there! Hey!"

Not my finest verbal offering, but then again, I'd never been in quite that predicament before. A situation I did not want to continue. So I shouted, or rather I bellowed for all I was worth.

Then I wondered how on earth they were going to find me, buried as I was in a hole in the ground. And how on earth did the snow not cave in on me before now?

As I shouted, I looked up and thought how I might attract attention from down there. I had bullets but no gun. I could set off a bit of gunpowder, but all that would do is flash and sizzle and smoke me out. Or take off some part of me I'd rather keep. No, I had to think of a different plan. One that ended up with me being alive, unburied, and with my head and arms still attached. So I kept on shouting and scrabbled around on the cold, dirt-rock floor for another stone to throw upward.

I reasoned that I might be able to lob it hard enough to dislodge some of the snow. Maybe it would cave in and, if I were lucky enough, it might pile up down here and give me a leg up in getting out. That would mean a whole lot of snow would have to fall and I'd have to be away from it while it did. I had no idea if that was even possible. I'd also likely have to do a whole lot of fancy jumping and climbing, and fast, as it fell.

First task first. I found a rock, probably the one I tossed upward last night—how it hadn't landed on my head, I'll never know—and with my left hand raised it back over my shoulder. It was an awkward pose, because it's tricky to throw straight up in the best of circumstances, and when you've been rolled and tumbled by a wall of snow and chucked in a rocky hole, you're not apt to be limber enough for tricky throws. I was not. I rethought my approach.

I cradled the rock in my left hand, cupped my right under it, and ignoring my throbbing, busted digit, I squatted low and as I rose I growled and shouted sounds that were not words. In a mighty and quick motion, I raised that stone up from between my ankles to knee height to chest height, and then I thrust that stone toward that glowing, snowy patch high above me.

It lodged there. It did not break through, it did not shatter the snow, it did nothing I wanted it to. On the contrary, it was now another thing that might fall on my head at some point. Great.

Then I heard the voices once more, and they sounded closer than they'd been. I resumed my imitation of a bull being branded, shouting sounds and, "Hey! Hey!" over and over. The voices stopped. Mine didn't.

I heard a clunking and a harsh dragging, scratching sound, then the world caved in on me.

CHAPTER TWENTY

This time the snow that dropped on me didn't pummel or crush me or seem to be out to kill me in any way. But it was annoying, a fact I overlooked once I got through shouting and pawing at the falling snow and looked up. I saw sudden light. Real light, not the foggy, blurry light from earlier. It was round, in the shape of my pit, and I realized it was the rim.

Straight above, I saw a blue sky with a long stretch of white cloud being pulled apart by a high-up wind. Something darker was angled over one edge of the hole. I don't know what it was, but it didn't move, not that I expected it to. But something else did move, a thin shadow that appeared to lean over the hole. It stretched further and further. Another appeared beside it, then another did the same from the other side.

The glow was still too bright on my light-deprived eyes. I narrowed them, then visored them with my hand. It helped, but not enough. All I saw were three or four less-than-shadowy shapes. Had to be people.

"Hey!" I said, figuring I had nothing to lose. "Hey up there!"

The shadowy sticks jerked back out of view, then angled in again. I heard noises, like low words being spoken back and forth. Snow fell down into the hole, not much but enough to make me jerk back. "Hey!" I shouted again. "You up there! Help me out of here, will you? Help!"

Again the figures retreated, knocking another dusting of snow into the hole.

"Hey!" I am nothing if not persistent. Why give up on a word because it scares people—if that's what they were?

I kept looking upward and was rewarded with one, two, three . . . at least four bumps creeping into the roundish space. They grew and grew and that's when I saw they were faces, human faces, staring down at me.

Then a voice said, "Notabear! Notabear!"

Or at least that's what it sounded like. He could have been saying he had no hair. Or "It's hot up here," neither of which made as much sense. Then it occurred to me I was wearing a big, shaggy, dark-haired coat and my head wore similar hair. Hmm. So yes, you could say that I was not a bear. But that would mean they had previously thought me a bear. I've been called a lot of things, but never a bear. Heck, I've been attacked by bears that obviously didn't think me one of their kind.

They kept it up, sort of a chant, over and over. Or maybe it was fanciful thinking on my part and it was a foreign language, perhaps French. I didn't know and I didn't much care. I wanted to get out of that freezing hole in the ground, and I needed their help to do it.

They looked down at me and now that my eyes were adjusted, I saw they were indeed people. Some of them had what I took to be long hair, dangling down over the edge of the hole. Light was blocked by my hand, by their heads, and by that weird jutting thing that now I saw might have been a rock.

They pulled back once more and I resumed my shouted pleas for assistance. It didn't take long for them to return, though. And within moments, I saw they were lowering something down the side of the hole.

I stepped back, uncertain as to what it was. It was girthy, bigger around than a man's head, maybe two heads, and it was lowering foot by foot toward me. As it slid closer, slowly, I figured it out. It was a log. And the closer it drew, the more relieved I became, because it wasn't just a log. It was a log with alternating wedge-shaped cuts on either side hewn into it. A ladder. They were lowering a ladder to me.

Where, I wondered, did they get a custom-made ladder? One that looked to be made for this hole? They weren't gone but a few minutes, not long enough to hew ladder steps into a log. That was all the time I spent dwelling on that thought, because I didn't much care where the ladder came from. It existed.

Still, as I reached for the log, questions popped into my mind, despite my efforts to not pay attention to them. What tribe were these people from? Did they dig this hole? For what purpose?

I steadied the log and guided it to a stop as they did the same up above, balancing it against the hole's edge. I made certain it was going to stay put and not roll too much. Then, with my hands holding it tight—still afraid it wasn't real, still afraid they might take it from me if it did prove to be my salvation—I shouted up, "Hey! Don't let go! Hold the top tight. I'm climbing up."

I didn't give the hole a single downward glance. Who would, after all, look back into their grave if they were given sudden life?

The log ladder's alternating cuts were smaller than I reckoned at first, and made for tricky climbing. It was all I could do, I found, to balance myself, compensating on my left side while my right raised up and sought purchase in the tiny, hewn step above. I slowly made my way up in that manner, right boot, left hand, left boot, right hand. That broken finger made for extra tough going, but I set my teeth tight and bulled on.

It was a poor job of balancing I got up to, but at least it worked. For about five feet. Then I heard the thing cracking and before I could do a thing about it, it sagged in the center, a bit further up-log of me, toward freedom. It swayed as it sagged, slowly giving up the ghost right there beneath me.

I'm not a small man, as I've said, and in a situation such as this it can be downright embarrassing to be me. I didn't much care what they thought, though. Instead, I put in extra effort. It wasn't pretty, me flopping and grunting and squealing and growling and scrambling to stay upright, move upward, not spin around to hang under the log, and to get on up to the top before the log snapped in two and dropped me back in the hole. It was a lot to muster and mostly it didn't work.

I was too busy climbing and working to not fall off the cracking log to look upward. So when I reached the rim of the hole, I was surprised. I clawed at the snow, hesitant to fully let go of the log, even if it was rapidly giving out, for fear I might not yet have a solid purchase on this higher-up terra firma. Well, snowa firma.

After much wriggling and thrashing, I found myself gasping for breath but relieved, with most of my body out of the hole and laid out on the snow. It took me a few moments to get over my elation and gather my frazzled senses. I rolled over onto my side, then flopped on my back.

As I gazed upward into bright sunlight, I blinked and squinted. Almost as if I were reexperiencing the scene on high from moments before down in the hole, I saw shapes, dark shapes, crowding into my circle of vision. I tried to rise, but the shapes recoiled, then shoved close all around me, a half dozen of them. And they were drawing closer. My turn to recoil.

I shoved backward with my elbows, but the faces shook side to side in a forbidding manner. I stopped, propped on my elbows, and got a better look at the faces as they crowded in, blocking out the bright sun. These faces were not like any I had ever seen. I saw now they were also sniffing the air about me, as if sizing me up as much by smell as by sight. Curious.

They were of a tribe, that much I saw, wearing ragtag clothes made of pelts. Many of the skins looked old, judging from worn-away patches. Poorly taken claws and teeth dangled down at me. The strange people leaned over me and since they were blocking out the light, I could see them more clearly. What I saw was the stuff of dreams. Bad, bad dreams.

CHAPTER TWENTY-ONE

They weren't human, couldn't be. Immediately I realized Jack's mad rants were true. These creatures, no other word for them, glared at me with intense curiosity and rage all at once. Beneath the flapping rags of ratty, matted furs hanging all about their heads and bodies, their eyes were red, bright red, brighter than fresh blood on snow, veined and popped and raw around the edges.

And their teeth, what I could see of them, for some of them had their mouths opened as if they were about to lunge down and take a bite of me, were blackened, ragged stumps, pointy ended and painful looking.

Their skin was dark, not like an Indian's or a Mexican's or that of the thin-as-a-whip escaped slave I'd met on the trail years before who called himself Sippy. He was the blackest man I'd ever met. His skin was pretty, like carved, polished wood with a glow beneath that shone like deep-fire coals. His kindness to me was unmatched at that point in my life, and his laugh was only rivaled, in richness and deep-down, gut-chuckling power, by Maple Jack's. But that's another story for another time.

The skin of these creatures staring down at me was dead black, though, and with no shine or glow of health. The closer they leaned down toward me, the more I saw of their faces, and those faces were filthy with crusted grime. I smelled woodsmoke, years of it, built up like layers, too much to ever scrape away.

Was filth their skin color?

That was all the time I had for such speculation because one of them, to my right, prodded me with a smooth-worn shaft of wood. The tip he jammed at me was sharpened to a point and it, too, was crusted, but with dried blood and hair. Of what or who, I knew not.

I made certain my hands were freed enough to snatch at the sticks should their poking become too aggressive for comfort. Their hands, wrapped about the shafts, I now saw, wore more of their wrapped flaps of furs and raw pelts. Some had dried nubs of shriveled flesh and sinew, indicating they were poorly cured, which would account for some of the awful stink.

They moved their faces closer, then backed away, and the claws and teeth and bits of whittled bone and wood clunked and rattled against the rest. I saw that many of these odd items, I assume worn for adornment, were woven into their long, matted hair as well.

I slowly moved backward, too, scooting to get my backside under me, bending my knees in case I had to lunge. I had no doubt that even with my heavy coat and layers of clothes beneath, they could pierce my hide should the urge grip them. As I did so, my coat, which had become mostly unbuttoned save for a couple of toggles down low, parted, revealing my layers of clothes beneath.

They gasped and shoved backward.

Again, I heard them murmur, "Notabear! Notabear!"

What I had assumed earlier was now proven true. They had thought, at least while I was down in the hole, roving beneath them in my fur coat and somewhat matted hair, that I resembled a bear. Odd they'd still thought that, after I'd bawled all manner of human words and had crawled up out of the hole.

I got the sense they were disappointed that I wasn't a bear. Me, too, sometimes.

They turned to stare at each other and mumbled low grunty sounds, some words, I thought, but I couldn't make them out. A couple of them coughed, deep-chested, rattly sounds, then they spat sloppily on the ground.

I couldn't help it. My eyes followed the gob, a yellow wad of phlegm on the snow. That didn't look healthy.

On cue, the others, one at a time, as if it were a contest or they'd been ordered to, coughed and worked up gobbets of spittle themselves and spat. Some of them worked it through their caked nostrils, too, then didn't bother to drag a foul hand under their noses or across their mouths. They let the strings of their phlegm hang.

It was enough to put even me off my feed. Might even be enough to put Jack off his jug. Then again, that may have been pushing it.

I took their skittishness as an opportunity to get my feet under me. Unfortunately, the notion I had in mind of springing to my feet, perhaps crouched and ready to pounce, agile as a cat, nimble like a deer, didn't match with what happened.

I grunted and lurched forward onto my knees, and managed to jerk one boot up, flat on the ground. I was still sore from my snowy beating, at least that's the lie I told myself to make myself feel better.

They backed off a pace or two, and I kept my eye on them, at least the ones before me. I figured there were two or three I couldn't see behind me, spears poised and those freaky red eyes wide with fear.

"Easy now, fellas," I said, holding up my hands in what I hoped was a gentling manner, as you do when you come upon a fetched-up horse. I didn't advance on them, but held my spot and shuffled my feet in a half turn, owling my head to see beyond me.

I sized them up as I turned. They were grimy and dark shapes against a backdrop of white snow, blazing with sunlight, so that I squinted. They didn't seem to have that problem. Might have been due to the stiff flaps of fur over their heads like hoods or bonnets. It was difficult to tell where their pelty robes ended and their own funky hides began.

Their hands were black, grimy things with long nails like claws. I've never seen fingernails as long on humans. Then again, I'd not decided they were human. What they were, I don't know. But their nails were begrimed in ways I could not begin to describe. And their feet, now that I was in a position to look them over, were the same, tipped with clawlike nails, long and gnarled and hard-yellow-black, with splits and chips in them.

This alone, the discovery that they were barefoot, told me I'd found, as if the red eyes hadn't done it, the culprits of the attack on Jack and Winter Woman. A detail came to me and I glanced again at their filthy feet. I noticed a puckered nub on one of them, between the yellowed, crusty, clawed toenails of his right foot, second smallest. So here was the very beast whose tracks I saw back at the cabin.

Any pinch of charity I may have felt for them having rescued me from the pit, which they likely dug—a clever yet simple means of animal trap, I admit—winked out like a snuffed candle as I fully accepted they were responsible for nearly killing my friend. And by relation, his friend, Winter Woman.

"Where is she?" I said, eyeing each of them as I slowly, ever so slowly, walked to my left, toward the big boulder that lorded over the uphill curve of the pit.

They didn't like my question or the fact that I was moving. They advanced on me, making those grunty, growly sounds low in their throats. I saw now they were a sorry lot, skinny and weak and weaving as they tried to make threatening motions toward me with the spears.

I also noticed the least bit of exertion on their part resulted in them wheezing and pulling in hard breaths, then letting out whistling sounds for their efforts. And then they repeated their coughing and spitting ritual, which, despite the vulgarity and disgusting sounds and sights it brought up, almost made me want to join in, if out of sympathy. But I recalled I had none for them. I made it to the boulder and kept it to my back.

This forced them to form a ragged circle about me, or rather about the pit. At this point I figured I could likely take them all on with my knife, but I wasn't one to bet. As weak as they looked and sounded, wheezing and blinking those cursed red eyes, I thought they still had enough strength in those bony arms to poke a few holes in me.

But not before I took them all out with a frontal attack using my big knife as a short sword and cudgel all in one.

CHAPTER TWENTY-TWO

For the moment, I held my anger and considered the boulder, thankful it sat where it did, affording me some meager protection. It wouldn't last, none of this could. The big, gray, rocky mass angled downhill, a jutting outthrust of stone as if it had been pinched and pulled backward like meringue by a giant hand.

How I managed to tumble by it and into the pit, of all places, instead of winding up downslope, covered over with snow, is a mystery to me to this day. The best I can think of is that the rushing snow shoved me forward below the rock. Maybe I had seen it and tried to make for the downhill edge of it, knowing it was my one hope since I couldn't outrun the avalanche. I had obviously been knocked on the head a bit, since I remembered nothing after seeing the wall of snow crushing down on me.

It was a jut of a drift, a skin of crusted snow no more than a foot thick at the downslope edge, and it appeared to taper uphill toward the boulder that I had somehow ended up below. It seemed against any notion of science that I should have fallen into the pit, but I did. And likely it saved my life.

I looked past some of the heathen beasts, northward along the slope, and saw that the far edge of the snowslide had been too far for me to outrun. There was a stand of stunted, yet still man-height pines and, from there and leading this way, I saw a fresh gouge, perhaps a foot wide, as if somebody had dragged something from there to here.

This puzzled me, and then I remembered the crudely carved log ladder they'd lowered down to me. My guess is they had built it some time before, probably years, given its dryness and urge to crack. It couldn't have been my weight on it, I told myself, not believing a word. That would have been how they climbed down into the pit once they'd driven their spears into the hole to dispatch whatever poor beast was unlucky enough to tumble in. I bet they baited it somehow, too.

How many such beasts had died a gruesome death in that very hole where I'd almost done the same? How many had bled out right where I'd sat, leaning and wondering what to do next? Rough way to go. I suppressed a shudder and regarded the mangy men once more. At least I thought they were men, though I still was uncertain.

"What's it going to be, then? You folks speak English? Huh?" I eyed them over. "English? Speak?"

Not a word but plenty of wide, red and yellow eyes giving me the same look-over. This was getting us nowhere.

Still they stood, occasionally glancing at one another as if they were communicating in silence. I waited, feigning impatience at first, then with genuine feeling. I decided to open the ball. Shoving off the rock, I stood fully upright and stretched, making as much of an indulgent, annoying, deep-voiced yawn as I could muster.

I stretched my arms wide over my head and ended the display with a headshake that had the opposite effect I intended, at least on me, as it dizzied me up some. I was still feeling less-than-impressive after my righteous snowy tumble.

The snot-addled brutes backed up another step and brandished their spears, jabbing the air and doing their best to menace me with their eyes. I am not a pretty man and I gave it back to them twofold. They appeared cowed somewhat.

"Look," I said, "I know you raided my friend and his lady

friend in their winter nest some miles downcountry from here. You made a holy mess of that place, tried your best to kill my friend, and made off with the woman. What I don't know is if she's still alive. I also don't know why you did what you did, nor what you think you're going to do with me. I also don't know if you can speak English. You've muttered a few sounds that could have been the word 'bear,' but . . ." I shrugged.

At my mention of *bear*, their foul eyes widened once more. I thought for certain that would set off another round of coughing and snotting, but instead they looked at each other again. I heard low, grumbly sounds and noticed, as I watched them, that the one in the middle of the seven men looked as if he was the leader of this little party. The others appeared to defer to him.

I believe they were all males, given their raggedy appearance and the lack of any shapeliness to their faces or bodies. The leader was not extraordinary, in fact he looked like the rest of them, that is to say, malnourished and grimy and altogether foul.

Finally, I got the impression they were waiting for me to make a move, and here I was waiting for them to do so. I said, "Okay, let's go." I set off toward the copse of trees from which they'd dragged the log ladder.

I can cover a pretty fair piece of ground when I have a head of steam built up. And that's what I did, despite the snow, not much concerned if they were going to stab me in the back. I glanced back a time or two and saw they were straggling and struggling to punch through the snow. How they managed to survive with their feet bare and their bodies draped in the most ragged of pelts, I'll never know.

I made it to the trees, looking hard at the slope down below us for sign of any of my gear. Of it I saw nothing, not a snapped snowshoe jutting from the crust, no sign of my fur hat waiting for me to snatch it up and shove it on my head once more. Not a corner of my backpack, no mittens, no sign of my Schofield revolver, or Sharps rifle.

For all my aversion to the deafening, cowardly ways of distant killing that guns represent, they are mighty useful tools for a variety of reasons, and the Schofield and Sharps had both been with me a long ol' time. I would miss them.

But my life was worth a whole lot more to me, and with each hole-punching step, I reminded myself I was still alive and able to walk on this stunning snowed slope, deep in the crystalline heart of the Shining Mountains in the early wintertime.

Sure, I was being trailed by sickly creatures the likes of which I'm fairly certain nobody on earth had ever clapped eyes on before. Yes, they were capable of great violence, as was made plain by Jack's stoved-in head and addled condition and by the mess the cabin was in. But I decided to make it to the trees, then I'd give them the chance to catch up.

I did, and glancing ahead through the sparse growth, I saw their trail punched through the tapered remnants of the slide of snow that had managed to leak down into the trees. Their path, the way they had come, led directly across the slope, straight beyond where I'd been walking.

I paused in the trees, grateful for the dappled shade they offered, for it gave my squinting eyes respite from the sun blazing down from above and from its glare off the snow.

"What's it to be, boys?" I said, raising my arms wide, then letting them fall. That hurt because I'd forgotten about my busted finger. It throbbed anew. I winced and decided not to let them see that I was ailing in any way. I also kept my coat unbuttoned, my knife in easy grabbing range should I find I'd misjudged them.

They straggled up near me, and with them came their stink. Oh, but it was rank. Wafting off them like the stench off green meat in the sun. Maybe worse.

I'd all but decided they were more human than not, when one of them hunched right up before me on the snow and relieved himself of whatever he'd eaten some hours earlier. The others paid him no heed until he stood and walked away, then they all glanced down at his leavings and appeared to sniff the air as a dog might the scat of another.

CHAPTER TWENTY-THREE

Whatever they were, they were far from the so-called civilized town dwellers I found in my far-ranging travels. Well, some of those town folk, anyway. Others of the settled masses were barely above brute behavior themselves, as evidenced each night in bordellos and saloons, howling and hooting and grunting their way through their paltry, shadowed lives.

No, give me the trail and fresh air and as true a companion as Tiny Boy, and Maple Jack on occasion, and I am more than satisfied. Towns, save for the convenience of buying supplies that I could do without, are little more than a nuisance to me.

Thoughts of Tiny Boy and Jack once more spurred me into action. I decided to continue following the red-eyed men's path back to wherever they'd emerged from. How far that would be, I had no idea, but the straggling creatures seemed to get the notion of my intention and doubled their efforts to keep up with me.

Soon they were poking me with tentative jabs, doing their best to surround me while we trudged through snow, now little more than a crusty scrim in most places on the sun-worked slope. They prodded me and I let them. If they got much bolder, though, I'd show them this non-bear would bite back.

They hunched and hopped and scowled and murmured, showing me, I believe, that they were indeed menacing. I didn't want to deny them their single, perhaps last, impressive attribute. Each move they made clinked and rattled their bones and fangs and teeth and claws and wooden bits tied to their garments and hair. And the more sound they each made with their trinkets, the more excited they became.

I studied on them some and could not figure out if they were Indians or half coyotes or some form of northern-dwelling brute descended from the far reaches of Canada, so tough did they appear with their bare feet and all. I did know without doubt they were unwell. That yellowness to their snottings, and the ragged, rattling coughs they got up to, were not something you'd see in any healthy critter, be it man or otherwise. But their breathing was audible and hard-won, as if each breath was close to their last.

Despite how foul they were and how much grief they had caused people I cared for, I couldn't bear listening to that breathing as they worked to keep up with me and show me they were menacing. So I slowed my pace.

If they were grateful, they didn't show it. Why would I expect such a thing? Must be the mountain air was getting to me. Heck, those red-eyed, crusty varmints weren't the only ones breathing hard.

As we walked along, my neck hairs bristled once more, and not because I was more or less surrounded by odd, sickly dog-men. It was the same crawling feeling I'd had before on this trip. A feeling of familiarity, of something, or someone, watching me from afar. Watching us, perhaps. Was it the wolves? Were they angry at being cheated of their near-prize?

I knew, somehow I knew, that I was being tailed up the mountains. I knew it then, when I first felt it, when I spun and caught that quick glimpse of . . . what? *What did you see, Roamer? Anything at all?*

The impulse, as we stomped along, seized me once more and I spun my head toward our backtrail. I saw something, I swear it. The odd creatures whose willing captive I was took little notice, save one.

Directly behind me, keeping a distance of perhaps ten feet, walked the one among them who the others had deferred to. He whipped his gaze behind us, too, as soon as he saw me do so. He may have seen whatever fleeting thing I'd caught a glimpse of.

We both stared in that direction for the span of a single step, perhaps two. He looked forward at me and this time, his gaze was anything but welcoming. There was hatred and rage in his eyes. And I guessed at what he thought: I had brought someone else. And this displeased him.

Well, fine. I hadn't, unless it was wolves. What of it? I was displeased, too. And a damn sight bigger than he was. I felt my knife's handle through my coat. It was untied and ready to grab. I did not like having him behind me. Not one bit. I credit the poor choice to my rough treatment by the elements. Usually, I am a little cleverer than that.

We walked on. I know that in their eyes I was acting more fidgety, and that's because I was. I stole glances back, and the leader met my glance each time, his red-eyed anger never waning. I matched it with my own. Despite the fact that I am not pleasant to look upon, no matter if I'm smiling or frowning, he was not cowed.

I sidestepped once and stopped, then motioned for him to go ahead of me. He stood hunched and breathing hard, staring me down. The rest of them halted, gasping and staring at me. He neither shook his head nor gave any indication he understood me. I took that to mean *no*.

Was I being led to my death at their hands? I was fairly confident I could lick them, but what if there were more? What if they had tricked me? They had already done so, in a manner of speaking, with the pit, after all.

I fell back into line before him and we resumed our walk.

CHAPTER TWENTY-FOUR

We'd been walking for hours through varied terrain, but always deeper, deeper into the mountains. For long minutes I'd marvel at the variety in the tree life, from stunty pines to stands of taller ponderosas, wondering at their tenacity at this elevation. Though it was still somewhat early in the winter, this high up, the blizzard of days before hadn't been the first of the season.

The depth of the snow I'd journeyed through on my snowshoes, and then afterward since I'd fallen in with the coyote men, crusted the entire mountainside and deepened the further we journeyed. And thus our pace slowed, owing to the increased snow and to fatigue. I did my best to pace myself, but I had nothing to sustain me, save for a packet of jerky in my coat pocket. I wasn't certain how the sight of food might set off these beasts, so I let it stay in my pocket. I could keep for a while longer without tucking into it.

I scooped snow regularly. Despite the fact that it chattered my teeth, I knew the benefits of staying wet on the inside, as Jack says, though his preferred solution comes from something else entirely. I was cold enough that I'd welcome a pull on Jack's jug, even though it could more often than not make a grown man howl like a paddled schoolchild.

The brutes ahead of me, though they breathed harder than ever and still struggled in the snow, kept up their pace. They walked low, hunched and with arms swinging so their filthy knuckles grazed the snow regularly, their spear tips wagging, the ends dragging. As to their bare feet, none of them appeared to be bothered by the cold. They trudged on, same as me. I admit I was impressed with their toughness.

In the midst of one of my moments admiring the surrounding mountainside, we began a descent, winding downward along a tree-shrouded canyon, a declivity that narrowed the lower we trekked. Finally, we leveled off and I noted how, though it was growing later in the day, we had lost much of the sunlight, not due to the sun sinking but because of the towering mountains rising like stark, craggy walls to either side of us.

The trees, while not growing tight, stippled the slopes and the canyon floor enough that they added to the gloomy scene, providing the final shade of melancholy I was fast beginning to feel.

I'm not normally a dour person, but this dark, dank place and the cold dwindling of the sunlight wore on me. The sounds of the beast men shuffling, their raspy, coughing breaths, wet with sickness coating their wheezes, their stench, all clouded about me as we walked. It mounded up and left me struggling to move forward, willingly subjecting myself to whatever it was they had in mind for me, wherever it was we were walking. It could surely be no better than this depressive trek.

At the moment I was about to halt, despite what I'd hoped would be the imminent discovery of Winter Woman's fate so close at hand, the creatures began slowing, clustering and walking in single file instead of the straggling, haggard clot of before. They slowed ahead and behind me, and I gave up breathing through my nose, hoping instead that their stink wouldn't contaminate my lungs. Their occasional grunts and gurgles became low, frantic, hushed whispers.

I thought perhaps I heard, once more, snatches of words that could be mistaken for . . . French? Maybe they were Métis? Or a remote tribe who'd had enough exposure to explorers or missionaries, possibly years earlier, that some of the language lingered somehow in their minds?

We now walked on a trail that seemed obvious because they led the way. Were I here on my own, I would have trouble guessing this was a path. Onward we walked into darker, shadowed space. Boulders appeared out of the low, pressing gloom, rising to head height. With the same one of them still behind me, I followed the rest into this rocky, hidden place, bells of alarm tolling in my head, as insistent as the sound of five churches on a Sunday morning.

Then we came to a narrow gap in an otherwise solid wall of boulders. Again, were I here on my own, I would have passed it by, considering it as all stone. The creature-men before me slipped through and I lost sight of them, so dark did it appear there. I made up my mind to give it up and savage the last of them, the one behind me, should he come at me. I stepped aside and there he was, closer than he'd been before. He glared at me with the same intense anger as earlier. Even in the gloom of that foul place I saw his fiendish, wet eyes.

That was all it took to amend my decision once more. My own unhappiness and discomfort were nothing compared with the pain and confusion he and his ilk had caused Maple Jack and Winter Woman. I might still be able to save her, somehow.

Keeping one eye on him and feeling my way forward, I bent down and stooped and turned sideways, edging through the stone gap in that manner, as it was slightly wider below head height of the others. Once I made it through, Ol' Anger Eyes quickly followed.

I straightened and looked about me. It was brighter than dusk, but gloomier than moments before. I found myself surrounded by stunty trees growing amid close-leaning boulders. The explanation was obvious—the rocks had collected here at the base of this mountain after crashing down from the heights lording above us, now invisible, concealed as they were in gray fog.

I resumed walking behind the creatures. A glance over my shoulder showed me Ol' Anger Eyes was still following. As we walked, I became aware of the increasing presence of markings on the stone faces, not like anything I'd ever seen before. Some were scratched in deeply, perhaps gouged with rocks. Others looked painted on with a thick, chalky substance. Still more were dark, red-black, and all of them looked troublesome. They were eerie—crude depictions of eyeballs and heads erupting like volcanoes and creatures that looked like bears or wolves or bison, I knew not which.

The stunty trees bore their own markings carved into their trunks, and their branches rattled in the dead air—how? I wondered—with poorly picked bones and teeth and whole skeletons of animals, from small, ratlike beasts, even mice, to the skulls of coyotes and mountain cats. I saw no human bones, at least none I was aware of. And then I did.

Propped atop some of the boulders were human skeletons. They were likely out of full eyesight of my traveling companions, but I was half again taller than them, perhaps less. It was difficult to tell, since they walked hunched over. At any rate, I saw the skeletons laid out on the rocks. Some of them bore puckered, dried, withered skin clinging to the bones. Shreds of hair danced in that same unfelt breeze, but their eyeholes were empty, their ribs little more than hollow bone baskets.

I assumed these were the coyote men's dead. I hoped so, since they all looked small. A couple of them were no larger than children. Further on I saw three, laid side by side, that were obviously small children, perhaps babies.

I have never been more depressed in my life. Nor more worried. What if some of the skeletons had belonged to people outside of this tribe, if indeed they were a tribe and if indeed they were people? I hadn't been convinced of either yet.

The way the skeletons were laid out on high reminded me a bit of the burial practices of the Lakota Sioux, who prop their dead atop tall pole scaffolds, wrapped in blankets and adorned with weapons and cherished possessions.

We kept on like this for many long minutes, winding our way through a stony gauntlet of gloom and bones. All the while, what light there was gradually diminished until everything about me, the beasts before me, the stones, all of it, took on a ghostly glow. Then we slowed.

If I had been uncharacteristically fearful before, what happened next made that trek with the snotting creature-men feel like a sunny day in summer, slumbering on a grassy field with a full picnic basket beside me.

This was anything but. This, I saw, as we stopped before a low, dark, craggy maw hacked into the solid stone of the mountainside itself, was their home.

CHAPTER TWENTY-FIVE

"That's about enough," I said, standing to one side of the gaping, black maw. Those who walked ahead of us paused inside the cave's toothy entrance. I kept them to my left and stared down at the menacing little troll behind me.

He doled out a big helping of smoldering rage with a low, growly sound from deep in his throat. It might have been more disturbing had it not been interrupted by a coughing spasm that wracked his bony body and hunched him up even smaller than he'd been before.

I wanted to laugh, but mocking another person's misfortune doesn't sit right with me, even if they aren't quite a person. "Look," I said. "I came here for the woman. Do you understand?" I gestured in the air before me, my big ham hands rendering the silly, curvy shapes men make in describing a woman.

I had no idea what size or shape Winter Woman came in, so I'm quite certain the glaring creature before me, having spat up a gobbet of yellow phlegm, his fellows following suit, had no notion of what my words or gestures meant.

He stared at me a bit more.

"Right," I said. "I've had it with you. I played the game, let you lead me here because I need to know of her whereabouts. But I'm done."

I glanced once more at the bony wraiths clustered at the mouth of the cave, shoved back the right side of my coat, and laid a hand on my knife. I had no idea if they knew I wore it. I'd never pulled it out in front of them, though neither did I hide its presence beneath my coat.

Two things happened then. My fingers closed on air, then patted the empty, useless leather sheath the knife normally rode in. I looked at the glaring creature. And he was smiling.

Smiling and holding my knife.

There was a moment when I must have looked as foolish as I felt, because he kept smiling. Then I must have looked as angry as I felt because his smile slipped. He grunted low like a bull calf and, silent as shadows, another half dozen of those skinny rascals appeared from all over the place, out from behind boulders, from atop them, out of shaded spaces between rocks. They'd been there the entire time. How many more were there? And how many more inside?

I stood there like the big goober I am, clenching and unclenching my useless hands, my busted digit throbbing like the head of a dunce under a too-tight hatband.

I offered up a growl of my own—far more menacing than anything those mucus-spitting bastards sent my way—and, bending low, entered the belly of the beast. That phrase kept echoing in my head as we wound our way inward.

My companions were not a silent lot at the best of times, but at least in the outdoors their grunts and coughs and spitting and hard, raspy breathing had been carried off on the cool mountain air. In the cave, the air was close and wet and dusty all at once, and the ragged walls were not hewn by human hands, I saw, but by ancient forces of nature who knows how long before. A thousand years? A million? No idea, but they were painful.

Whenever I dared raise my head as we walked, I was rewarded with sharp knocks and piercings and jabs of pain as my bean met the knobs and jags of the cave wall and ceiling. There was no light save for a persistent dull, yellow glow from rocks all about us, as if the cave itself were alive and leaking a paltry amount of sunlight it had somehow stored up.

I've been in mines, even worked in one for a week, until I became bedeviled by the notion that an entire mountain squatted above me, pressing down on me, and could give up the ghost any time at all and collapse on me like a pole-axed steer. But somehow this time it was all much worse. Nothing I told myself made a difference.

It didn't help that the grimy little leader was grunting and hacking along right behind me with a spear and my sharp-as-hell knife. He held it ready to poke through my big buffalo hide coat and slide between my ribs, making a gash wide enough for my innards to gush out.

The meager glow was enough to detect shapes before me, but not enough to prevent me from rapping my head over and over again. My hands helped, outstretched and grasping and patting the air like a blind man will do. They ended up cut and bleeding, and the busted finger jammed up hard a number of times against juts of stone. I stifled more than a few groans.

Sometimes those before me seemed to disappear, then I'd see a shadowy movement to my left or right. I learned quickly that we were in a network of passages. I was beginning to doubt my abilities to find my way out again when I managed to get free of these devious little demons.

At first, I thought I could memorize the turns somehow— left, left, right, left, sharp right—but it was a fool's hope. Even if I could remember, I'd have to recall them in reverse order. I gave up the idea as a waste of time and concentrated on besting these creatures. They likely hadn't killed me yet because they didn't want to have to haul me to wherever it was they were leading me. Their home, I assumed, deep in the beast's belly.

How much farther? And what would they want of me once

we reached their destination? I assumed it had something to do with food, with cannibalism. I'd rather admit the grim truth and prepare for it than be a cud-chewing lamb at slaughter time. If that was their aim, why hadn't they taken Jack? That thought almost made me smile. I couldn't imagine Jack trussed up like a dressed hog, rotating slowly on a spit over a fire. Too tough to gnaw through is the likely reason they left his curmudgeonly old hide behind.

At any rate, I was certain this tribe was not the sort to let people go, secretive as they were. Had anyone ever found them before? And what of Winter Woman? Was she here? Was she still alive? And why take her? But I knew. Or at least I'd formed a solid idea upon meeting them. They were sickly and, somehow, they knew she was a healer. How they knew such a thing was beyond my ken at that moment. Nor did I care. But it answered a stack of questions. Not enough to satisfy me.

And so we trudged deeper, deeper, into the belly of the beast.

CHAPTER TWENTY-SIX

The stink off the creatures had built in its foul intensity since we entered the caves. It made a poor situation much worse because of the added presence of more of them, the ones who'd oozed into sight at the entrance. I also saw more of the man-beasts ahead, or at least of their hunched little shapes lurching ahead of me along a path they obviously knew well.

The increased stench forced me to breathe solely through my mouth. It helped. Not a lot, but I took any relief at that moment. When I first met them, what rolled off them had been the stink of unwashed bodies, dirty hair, and layers of caked grime. But in the cave, it became the stink of death. The sweet, rotting-meat stink of decaying corpses.

The deeper in we walked, the more I realized the light had begun to slowly, step by wretched step, increase in equal, though opposing, amounts to the stink.

We low-walked at a trudge through the sometimes elbow-tight passages for what felt to be the better part of an hour, though I got the feeling we'd been traveling in circles—perhaps to confuse me? Then I heard a noise beyond the usual coughs and ragged breaths. It was deep and full, as if many thin sounds were combining to make this sonorous tone. On we walked. The sound grew louder. Yes, I knew it for what it was now. Voices, murmuring together, louder and louder.

The volume rose, the stink grew, and the creature-men before me quickened their pace and gabbled low to each other, slap-

ping their hands against their fellows' shoulders in what I took
to be excitement. I imagined the same happened behind me. I
didn't look back. I'd done so a few times and saw the same
thing—the leader creature eyeing me, my knife poised, others
behind him crouched and advancing.

Ahead, we cornered left and the light grew much brighter.
Then the stony passage ended and we emerged into a vast
chamber. I paused and took it all in. For what I saw was a most
incredible sight, one of the strangest in my thus-far somewhat
strange life.

About two dozen more of those creature-people stood,
leaned, or sat scattered about the room. They were similar in
appearance to those who brought me here—haggard and grimy,
covered in greasy soot. Their clothes, if that's what they could
be called, were little more than rotting strips of mangy animal
hide that hung on their gaunt, gasping bodies.

The ceiling was fifteen to twenty feet high at the center,
beneath which a decent fire burned. Whatever they were burning was not wood, for the smell was bitter and the smoke it
produced was thick and black. The room was not as smoke-
filled as I expected, though it was choking enough to force a
cough from me. But the smoke had to be going somewhere,
leaking upward through a fissure in the mountain of rock above,
I expect.

I felt a none-too-gentle prod at my shoulder and angled
myself to my right, taking in the one behind me, the beast with
my knife. He'd jammed me with the point of his spear to get
me to move forward. I did not comply.

I stepped quickly to my left, leaning forward to accommodate
the curve of the ceiling's upward slope. I hugged there, my back
to the wall. I wasn't about to wander to the cookfire and prep
myself for slaughter.

He surprised me then by not giving me his customary surly

look. Instead, he shrugged and ambled past me, as did his fellows, and joined the rest of the group. They drifted into the mass, approaching others of their kind and communicating in low murmured sounds. I could not make out if they were words. I assumed those they greeted were their family members.

I recalled seeing packs of coyotes doing much the same, nipping and rolling and frolicking and growling with each other in a friendly manner. I couldn't say these brutes were all that friendly to each other, but there was a general sense of familiarity among them. A relaxation of some sort.

Oddly enough, very few of them paid me much attention, neither those I'd not seen before then, nor the ones who hauled me in here. Then they began sniffing the air, though what they expected to smell other than the stink of the place—unwashed critter, dung, rotten meat, an odd, greasy smoky stink, and other scents too foul and strange for me to identify—I had no idea.

One by one they turned their heads toward me, and their squinty red eyes opened wide. "Bear! Bear!" they said in ragged unison as they stumbled backward.

The one who'd stolen my knife shuffled out between them and me and shook his head. "Notabear! Notabear!"

I think he intended this to be a shout, but his voice was hoarse from coughing and breathing so hard. He shuffled toward me and pointed with his spear, pawed at the air by his own midsection, and then jerked his chin toward me.

I took that to mean he wanted me to part my coat to show I was, indeed, not a bear. I had half a mind to tell him to go to hell and cinch my coat tighter. Maybe having some of them think I was a bear might give me an edge on them, somehow.

Then I wondered if he would come at me and poke me with that damned stick. Suddenly, the possible advantages I imagined in keeping the coat closed tight withered. I was bone-tired and sick of these creatures. I wanted to find Winter Woman and somehow force them to get us back out of there.

One moment, none of it seemed possible. Then the next moment, I thought of Jack, withered and skittish and backed into the corner, gibbering and crazed. That's when I felt I could make them do anything I wanted. First, I would play along. I stepped forward so I could stand fully upright, then I parted my coat. I stretched my arms wide and let out a loud, deep growl of frustration and anger. It was fun. And it worked.

The filthy creatures, men, women, little ones, all stumbled backward, the knife thief included.

"Ha!" I said, clapping my hands together. "Take that, you . . ." Then I saw the genuine fear in those sad, sickly faces and I shut my mouth. Whatever they were, they were not wholly menacing to me, at least not yet. Yes, they'd done wrong by my friend and his woman, but more and more, I realized it was desperation that drove them to it. I'd hold my tongue, along with further uncharitable thoughts about them, at least until I learned the truth.

I glanced back down the passage from which we came and was tempted for a long moment to bolt into it. Then I realized why they let me be. They knew the passages, the way out. I did not. I bet I could be lost forever and a day in there and never find my way outside. I'd die of starvation—or cuts to my head from the jagged ceiling—long before I found my way to fresh air again on my own.

No, I realized as I shifted my gaze from the darkening tunnel back to the domed chamber full of odd, wolfish creatures more beast than human, I was well and truly stuck. I also noticed they were all still looking at me.

I stared back, not certain what was about to happen. If they rushed me, I had two options, and I had to exploit them both at the same time: Run back down the passage, hoping for the best.

And as I ran, I had to pull out my trusty folding knife, the Barlow I've carried for years. It's never let me down, though there is always room for a first time in life. But I didn't need to make that happen. At least not yet. The group of haggard creature-people stepped away from their loose cluster about the fire, dragging lame feet, struggling and tugging their youngsters. And there were a number of miniaturized versions of the older creatures, equally hollow-eyed and grimy and so thin to look on it was painful.

When they stopped, pressed back against the curved walls of the space, I realized there was another of them across the fire, opposite me. He was larger than the rest and sat on a stone chair of sorts, elevated several feet above the floor. And he stared at me.

There was something about him that made me stare back, which I did for a long moment. And then I knew what it was. He was a she.

CHAPTER TWENTY-SEVEN

That's when I saw that she was not like the rest of them. She was plump, had long, dark hair, a round face, a round body, and a mix of anger and fear on her not-quite-grimy face. Her clothes were unlike those of the rest—they were a mix of buckskins and skirts of woven cloth, colorful even in the dim, smoky chamber. Her feet wore thick moccasins. But it was what she wore around her wrists and across her belly that I took interest in. It was vines, coarse-woven and lashed about her.

It had to be Winter Woman.

"Who are you?" I said, at the same time she said it.

I beat her to the answer. "Maple Jack sent me." I wanted to see if my guess was correct. Judging from the relief that spread across her face, I'd say I was right.

"Jack is alive?" She fairly shouted it.

I nodded. I wanted to say more but I did not know how much these cave dwellers could understand. "Are you okay?"

She nodded. "Yes, now I am."

That meant she was relieved Jack was alive, good, but I needed to know if she'd been harmed. "Are you hurt?"

She shook her head *no*. "I am tied, but they are afraid."

"Afraid? Of what?"

Before she could reply, the knife thief grunted and waved his arms, shaking his head to shut us up. I wanted to drive a fist in his face, but I'd need him or the help of those he controlled in order to get Winter Woman out of here. I'd wait out my chance.

I stepped forward. "I want to talk with her." I jerked my chin toward Winter Woman. "Now."

The knife thief scowled at me. It didn't work any better than it did last time. I leaned close to him. The stink was awful, but I gritted my teeth and flicked a finger in his face. "Don't push your luck, little man."

I'm not normally one to take advantage of the fact that I'm larger than your average fellow, but sometimes that's too bad. My bullying posture worked. While he didn't ever look particularly frightened, not as much as I wanted him to, he did seem to consider what I was asking. Then I swear he almost smiled as he stepped to the side.

I took that as an invitation and stepped toward the bound woman. As I did, the rest of the bony wretches skittered away from me, their red and yellow eyes wide, their breathing and coughing no different than that of the ones I'd let bring me here. All but one of them.

Knife Thief stepped before me with more speed than he'd shown since I made his foul acquaintance. He held out a hand, palm up, leaned forward, and blew on it.

A cloud of dust puffed at my face. I smelled his rancid breath even as I jerked away. I pawed at the cloudy mess, aware my eyes were watering.

A woman's voice shouted loud words that began as, "No! Do not do that!" and ended in a muddied slurry of sound as I staggered and coughed and pulled at my coat collar and long-handle shirt to wipe my face.

The cave wall met the side of my head and felt as though it punched a hole in my skull. I reeled, and sudden illness draped itself over me like a wet wool blanket.

The shouting continued. What had been a woman's voice was now a volley of cannon fire that I knew, somehow, was still a human voice. But the words echoed and pinged and slammed off each other, off red-rock canyon walls deep down on a hot day, but cool at the base of the dry wash I felt myself in. I staggered forward, aware that whatever had been in my gut so many hours before, whenever I last ate, was now happily forcing itself up and out.

What was happening to me? While that thought nibbled at me, others, hundreds, thousands of odd thoughts, memories, smells, sounds, feelings jerked at me from all sides. I spun, at least I think I did, and felt something else slamming into my head, my shoulders. I dropped to a knee and tried to remain upright, but somehow some great brute of the skies spun the earth, and the ground beneath me grew more interested in becoming the sky.

I fell sideways, hit something else sharp, and forced my eyes to open wide. That may have been a mistake, for I saw faces. Lots and lots of faces. But they were not faces I had ever seen, nor were they faces I ever cared to see again. They appeared to be made of melting tallow, dripping sizzling black wads of fat on me even as they howled and leered, closing in on me from above. Their mouths, formless black holes, chanted, "Notabear . . . Notabear . . . Notabear . . ."

I swatted and pawed at them, I struggled, I clawed the air, but they kept coming, gibbering and then gnashing at me with long, sharp teeth the color of disease, of oozing pustules. Bad as that was, it was the eyes that got to me, at first hollows of blackness that huffed smoke, holes in a barren ground, that flicked open inches from my face. Then the eyes were ragged green sores in the centers, with bloody veins trailing outward like sudden rain in a parched land, seeking cracks in the earth. But the rain was blood, hot, blood, and it pelted down with sizzling fury, burning holes in my head, my arms, my shoulders.

I held up my hands to stop it, but the bloody rain burned through them. I held a hand before my eyes and saw a dozen holes, and still the rain came down.

All this time the faces leered closer, gnashing and howling and doing their best to feast on my flesh, chanting, "Notabear! Notabear! Notabear!"

Somehow, I knew I was in a hell from which I would never escape. Sounds crashed and slammed about me, hundreds of fists pummeled me, and the stink of a thousand-thousand rotting battlefield corpses filled my nostrils, and on and on it went.

I heard a high sound cutting above, through the rest of the din of this hellish place where I was trapped. The other sounds fell away and that one sound remained, louder with each passing moment, until I recognized it for what it was—a human voice. But it was the voice of desperation, the victim of a torture so deep and relentless and intense that all other sounds in the world bowed to it, were stilled by it, and listened, afraid.

It was, I became aware, my own voice. The voice I'd used all my life, for good or ill, but now it was doing something I'd rarely heard, perhaps had never heard from myself. It was a full-throated scream, a never-ending shriek of terror.

Then it pinched out and nothing but blackness remained.

CHAPTER TWENTY-EIGHT

"Hey! Hey, mister . . ."

Something patted me on the face.

"Hey, mister!"

It patted harder, maybe it smacked me.

"Hey!"

Yep, definitely slapping me. I did my best to move aside, to tell whoever it was to knock it off. The way I felt, as if a cannonade were thudding inside and outside my head, I didn't need anyone whomping on me. The words I chose were, "Stop it!" I am, after all, a man modest in speech, if not in thought.

What came out, however, was a dry, croaking sound. Then I vomited. Or rather, my body tried to. My rib cage spasmed and bucked and sharp pains stabbed up my throat.

"Do not try to talk. Be still and drink this."

It was a woman's voice. Then I felt warm liquid slide over my lips. A hand pried my lips apart, forcing my jaws wider. I realized I'd been clenching my teeth tight together.

"Easy now," she said, and then I relaxed enough, must have, because I felt the liquid drizzle into my mouth. It stopped partway down my throat. I gagged and spat up the water.

"That's good, now your throat will work once more."

And she was right. My throat did work. She poured more of the warm liquid into my mouth and I kept it down. It soothed me inside, all the way into my body, giving me enough strength to do the thing I hadn't known I'd been trying to do the entire time—open my eyes. They flicked open and though I saw little save for dim, blurry shapes, my vision soon sharpened.

Leaning close was the face of a stout woman, kindly seeming, but unsmiling. "You are Jack's friend," she said.

I was about to say the same. Instead, I tried to nod, and ended up croaking out, "Yes. Roamer. My name's . . ."

She nodded. "Roamer. Jack talks much of you. He calls you his son, but he says you are closer than that."

She said it as a matter of fact, and even in my odd condition, it brought a quick lump to my throat.

"They hit him on his head. They would not let me help him."

I tried to sit up. She helped me and, after much grunting and moaning, I sat leaning against a rock wall. "I found him. He was pretty sore, but when I left him, he was much better." I hope my thin lie was convincing. In truth, I was worried about Jack and regretted my decision to leave him.

"That is good."

I heard a grunt from the shadows. There was Knife Thief, squatting by the door of the cavern.

"Where am . . . oh, yeah," I said, the situation tumbling back into my mind.

She offered me more water, but I shook my head. "Not just now, thanks. It's terrible stuff."

"Yes, but it is all we will have."

"What did he do to me?" I eyed Knife Thief, who grunted again, but kept his distance. The rest of them appeared to take our presence as normal and resumed their weak, low mumbling.

She shrugged. "He thought you were going to attack me. He blew the powder of the rot root in your face. They did the same to Jack. It causes madness."

"I'll say."

"It lasts longer in most people. But you are big and strong of mind."

I rubbed my aching head. "If that's a compliment . . . thanks."

"It was not meant to be."

I glanced at her. She was a curious thing. "When I first saw you, you were tied. Why?"

"It was not tight. I could free myself."

"Then why didn't you?"

"And do what? I cannot leave. They untie me when they need my help. It gives them a feeling of power."

"Is that why they brought you here?"

She sighed and nodded. "I am a healer. They are all sick. Their healer, I think she was also their leader, she died."

This was interesting, though some of it I had guessed. Not the bit about their leader, nor the leader being a woman. "What tribe are they?"

She shrugged. "They know some English. They call me 'Mama Rutha.' " Winter Woman shook her head. "I do not know who this is. Maybe it is that woman who died. I think they want me to be this person, but I am already a person. I cannot be another."

"Did they say anything else?" I said, eyeing the leaning guard by the chamber's entrance.

She nodded. "Yes, many things."

I wondered what they could have related to her. Perhaps some clue as to who they were, where they were from, and why they lived in a dank cave filled with stink, greasy smoke, and bad light.

She'd gone silent for the moment, but I wanted answers to a hundred questions. I tried to get her chatting again. "May I ask your name?"

She shrugged. "Call me what you like. To Jack, I am Winter Woman." She offered a slight smile. "Mostly 'Woman.' To my parents, I was called something else. To me, I am me."

I was beginning to learn she was a deep pool, a person with

much to offer, given time. How much time would we have, lost under the mountain? I certainly understood keeping oneself to oneself. I didn't pester her with another personal question. As it happened, our budding conversation was cut short as Knife Thief closed in.

CHAPTER TWENTY-NINE

He walked up to Winter Woman and pointed his spear at her, then jerked his head over his shoulder. While he did this, another of them, what I believe was a female, smaller and thinner than Knife Thief, busied herself working to loosen, with trembling, clawing hands, the rest of the wrappings that encircled Winter Woman's waist and trailed to the stone seat close by.

Winter Woman rose and smoothed her ample skirts.

Anger mixed with fear jolted me. "Where are you taking her?"

She laid a hand on my arm. "It is all right. I go to help the sick."

"With what?"

I think that offended her, because she looked at me as if I'd belched in church, then tapped her temple. As they led her from the chamber, she said, "I will be back." She left, followed by the few other cave dwellers who remained.

I made to follow her, but Knife Thief growled and poked at me with the spear, not touching me, but not endearing himself to me, either.

"Okay, little man. You win, for now."

Still dizzy, I leaned against the boulder beside the stone chair Winter Woman had occupied. He regarded me a moment, then backed away, dragging his feet, as if the act of walking took most of his scant strength.

Soon the cloying heat made me drowsy. It didn't help that I'd begun the day in a hole in the ground I'd been shoved into by a mountain of snow. Then we'd walked for what felt like weeks, with no sustenance save for scooped snow. I wished I had some with me now, to cool my face and wet my throat. I'd avoid their water until I had to take in more. Given the state of the place, I would wait as long as possible before asking for a drink. That liquid of theirs was fetid, sludgy, and foul.

As I did not wish to doze off before Knife Thief, subjecting myself to whatever it was he had in mind for me, maybe more of that damnable powder, I shrugged out of my heavy buffalo-hide coat. I am always surprised how much it weighs. It's akin to carrying a half-grown buffalo on my back.

I had forgotten he was watching. His raspy gasp reminded me. I looked at him and saw the wide eyes of someone astonished. The coat, of course. He stared at it, then me, then the coat.

"It's just a coat," I said, tugging my layers of shirts. "See?"

His eyes narrowed once more, and he glanced to the side, as if to dismiss his previous reaction. He could also have been looking toward someone else. Considering how secretive these creatures were, there were likely more of them lurking in the shadows.

As I folded the great wad of hair-coat, then rolled it roughly in half, my beloved, battered copy of the Thoreau's *Walden* slipped out of its inner pocket and landed at my feet.

Knife Thief gasped and scurried forward. I snatched up the book before his spear point landed on it. But he didn't thrust at it. Rather, he pointed toward it, even as I lifted it and held it close to my chest, keeping one arm free.

His eyes were wide and his breathing shallow. He stared at the book, then after a few moments looked up at me, an odd expression of—what? Expectation? Surprise? Hopefulness?—appearing on his face.

"It's a book," I said, hefting the volume. "Book."

He leaned forward, his lips parted, his brow drawn. He nodded as if he knew what I meant, and looked for all the world as if he were a hungry stranger coming upon a food strange to him, but wishing nonetheless to sample it.

"Book," I repeated.

"Boo . . ."

"Yeah, close. Book." I said it slower. "Boo-oo-k."

"Boo-g-g." His voice was a hoarse, creaky whisper.

"Not bad," I said.

He stared at it a few moments more, then met my eyes again. This time, though, the rheumy rage of before was replaced with scrutiny. He was thinking. I got the sense it was momentous, as if he were deliberating whether to decide something.

I said, "Book," once more, but he was turning away. I'd nearly decided to jump him. That nightmare powder episode wasn't something I would easily forget or forgive. Likely never would.

He'd not yet turned his back on me, at least not with us being alone. But then what? I didn't know how far away Winter Woman was, nor what direction would lead to freedom. I dithered and my opportunity vanished.

He resumed his station by the door and I tucked the book back into my coat's inner pocket. It was too dark to read in the cave, anyway. But he regarded me for a long time and I got the sense he was coming to that decision. About what, I had no thought.

As sore and as tired as I was, I must have dozed some time after that, because I came to in time to see Winter Woman returning to the chamber. Knife Thief walked behind her with that silly spear until she took her seat on the rock.

I stood and waited, ready to interrupt should another of them try to tie her up once more. But he surprised me by glancing at me, then retreating back to the doorway of the chamber, twenty or so feet away. He didn't glower.

"What's wrong with them?" I asked her, leaning close.

"They are fevered." She patted her chest. "With a sickness deep in here. I would have brought my tinctures, but they did not let me when they took me and hurt Jack."

"They shot themselves in the foot, all right."

Her look told me she did not understand.

"They ruined it for themselves."

"Yes, yes," she said, rubbing her eyes. She looked tired. I needed to get her out of there and we had to act fast. Every minute wasted was a minute we'd become weaker from lack of food and drink. I'm no doctor, but I know enough about healing and illness to know we were setting ourselves up for catching whatever creeping filth had inflicted itself on their lungs. I wanted none of it.

"Ma'am, we have to get out of here. Do you understand? The sooner the better."

She surprised me by shaking her head. "No, they need help. My help."

"That's admirable, ma'am, but it's not reasonable. We stay here much longer and we're liable to wind up like them—small and weak and sickly. That isn't something Jack would want for you. Besides, they're dangerous. Look what they did to Jack."

That gave her pause. Might be that wasn't a fair thing to say, but I didn't care. Time was precious.

Still, she surprised me by shaking her head again. "No. I am a healer. My place is here. I have to try."

I sighed. Maybe another approach would work better. "What else do you know about them? You hinted earlier at knowing more than you said."

"Yes, I have learned things about them. They are a sad people. They have been here a long, long time. How long, I do not know. Many, many seasons. I think they are from a large group of travelers, holy people trapped here in the Shining Mountains.

They were starving when they found this cave. There was food here. Animals, wolves, I think. But I could not understand what it was they were saying. Maybe coyotes."

"How did you find all this out?" I asked.

She gestured at the slouching Knife Thief. "Not from him." Then she grinned. "From the women, always it is the women who carry on the stories." She tapped her temple again. I was beginning to see how she could be a match for wily Maple Jack. She was a mischievous one.

"Well, did the women tell you anything else?"

"They were sick when they came here. The sickness they have now. It goes away, sometimes for many seasons. When it comes back, it is bad and people die. Each time it comes back, it is worse. They are worried for their children."

"I don't blame them. Those kids looked pretty rough." I thought back to the skeletons we passed on the way in, particularly those that were child-sized. It was a brutal thought that more would likely join them.

"They were shunned by the rest in the traveling group."

"A wagon train?"

She nodded. "I think so."

"Who would do such a thing to their fellows? And worse, why would these people stay here? Why not leave once the winter was over with? Surely they had the ability to walk on out of here. Couldn't be any worse on the trail than living like this."

"It is easy to say. But they were told by the first Mama Rutha, as they called her, many women ago, that the world was evil and if they went out into it, they would succumb to a sickness of the devil that would take them down into the earth where they would burn forever."

"Sounds like those tetched-in-the-head, fire-and-brimstone preachers I've run across in my travels. Never happy until they make everyone around them fearful and skittish. But how could these folks lose their language, their ability to act and think like humans?"

Winter Woman looked at me hard. "It does not take long for people to go back to what they are inside." She rapped her chest, then tapped her head, her arms, her legs. "Inside we are all as the wolf."

"Mm-hmm." I nodded. "Animals at heart."

This was fascinating and frightening, all at once. The notion of us all being base creatures down deep was something I did not disagree with. I'd seen too many instances of men drinking too much and then savaging their families, prostitutes, the town, stray dogs, their horses, themselves, anybody and anything they felt to be a challenge.

But that's where we differ from the other animals of the world. Humans debase themselves because they can. Animals never act anything more or less than what they are. Maybe wild animals react, defend, snarl to keep threats at bay. Humans tend to become their own threats.

If what Winter Woman heard was true, I wondered how long they'd been there in the mountains. Whites pounded the way west a whole lot earlier than those Clark and Lewis fellows on their mapping expedition. But how long would it take for people to lose whatever scrap of humanity they'd had? Was it a wagon train of religious folks taking their beliefs westward to preach to what they called the "heathens"? If so, it was a mighty slice of irony at play here.

I have no problems with folks wanting to pray to whatever god or God they choose. Have at it, but don't push it on me without my invitation to do so. But I hold little warm thought for the zealots among them. Especially those who claim their beliefs are the final word on the matter. This disavows religions from all over the world that have been around far longer than Christianity.

I'm bothered to my bones when I hear of, or worse, see those thumpers storm into the wilderness and scream their holy rage in the faces of some tribe that's been worshipping its various assortment of deities for thousands of years, and doing so quite happily.

If that is truly what this little clot of stunted cave dwellers had been, over time they apparently committed all manner of odd affronts holed up in the ground, starting with fornication amongst themselves. I don't know how many members their initial group held, but judging from the number of dead and sickly youngsters, they were having increasing trouble keeping their population, and their health, up. They were on the wrong half of a losing game.

Winter Woman surprised me then. "Until I learned this about them, I believed them to be the Alooknok."

CHAPTER THIRTY

"Alooknok?" I said, though I knew the word, had known, in fact, before Jack had mentioned it.

She nodded. "I am certain you know of what I speak, but I will tell you what I know." She swallowed, closed her eyes, smoothed her coat and skirts on her lap, and rested her hands flat on the tops of her legs. Then she spoke.

"A long time ago, long before the earth was the earth, there was Pouk. Pouk was not man, not woman. Pouk was. Pouk was alone and grew lonely from this, so Pouk reached into itself and pulled out a great light that glowed and twisted and turned in Pouk's hands, growing larger now that it was no longer locked inside Pouk. Soon it was as big as it could get and so Pouk released it and it became. But Pouk was dissatisfied.

"The ball glowed light, nothing more. So Pouk patted it and the light softened. Still Pouk was not satisfied. Pouk spit on the dull ball and parts of the light became the great water. It was better, but not good enough, decided Pouk. So Pouk reached inside and pulled out a great handful of dust, then blew on it, and it swirled over the light and water and this became earth.

"Then Pouk breathed on what was created and it became the skies. After all that, Pouk was still lonely, and cried, and Pouk's tears dripped down Pouk's long nose and onto the swirling ball of light and air and water and earth. The tears dripped through the light and air and pelted the earth and the water. Where they hit, green trees and grasses and flowers bloomed and fish took

165

shape and creatures emerged from the dust and dirt, covered with hair and feathers.

"Pouk was less lonely as Pouk watched the creations come alive. But over time it was not enough. Pouk was still sad, and then angry for having wasted so much time on creating foolishness. Pouk raised a great hand into the air to strike a killing blow down on the living ball. Pouk drove that fist deep into it, to the very core of it. But instead of destroying it, all the rage in that hand, that weapon of anger, released into the heart of the ball.

"On seeing what the blow had done, Pouk felt great shame and pity and withdrew the hand of anger. But it was too late. All of that sadness and rage had been left behind in the center of it.

"On seeing that the ball could not be destroyed, Pouk worried for the creatures in the water and in the air and on the land, and whispered soothing words that settled on the ball as gentle breezes. At the same time, the anger boiled and churned in the middle of the ball and found its way to the surface and poked through the land.

"When it did, it was met with the kindness of the gentle words, the breezes. The good and the bad fought and fought and one could not win over the other. Soon they were so mixed up with one another that they could not remember what it was they were fighting about, and became one tired and angry and happy and kind and evil creature. These became people."

Winter Woman stopped speaking.

I realized I, too, had closed my eyes. I opened them to find her looking at me.

"It's a good story," I said. "You tell it well." And I meant it, even though it did not tell me what an Alooknok really was.

She must have seen the question on my face because, for the first time since I'd met her, Winter Woman smiled. "Jack chose well when he chose you as a friend." She closed her eyes once more and I vowed to keep mine open this time. I couldn't let her storytelling lull me into forgetting where we were, nor who kept us there.

"Finally, with people running all over the world that Pouk created, Pouk was no longer sad or lonely. Times were good and the people were happy, too, with Pouk to talk to and the animals to live with and the plants and fish and bees and flowers and birds. But this did not last forever. For not all of the anger and rage and hatred and misery was gone from the center of the world. Some of it had remained. And it was not happy at all.

"It finally found a way to escape from the center of the world, and it did. It emerged at night when all the people and creatures were asleep and Pouk was not paying attention. Where did it emerge? In an unknown cave deep in the mountains, a dark place never seen by animals or people. The first creatures the anger came upon were a pack of sleeping wolves.

"Before they could awaken, the anger seeped into them and turned them savage, sour, rotten. They lived for a long, long time, venturing out from the secret cave late in the nights, attacking and spreading the anger and evil and malice, then retreating to the cave before dawn. This went on and on.

"Eventually, Pouk noticed that this happy earth was not as happy as it once had been. The people were bickering and acting oddly, running from the animals instead of talking with them. The animals and fishes and birds all did the same. Then they began fighting among themselves. This alarmed Pouk and Pouk decided to do something about it, though what, Pouk did not yet know. Pouk was confused, as the anger and rage and malice seemed to have been conquered once the people emerged. Pouk decided to watch and wait to try to find the cause of all this new anger.

"It took many, many days and nights before Pouk saw the

dark, thin shapes of the angry wolves appear in a forest. They were so thin, they looked like little more than black shadows in the dark. But Pouk saw them move toward sleeping creatures, people and bears and rabbits. Before the wolves appeared, the slumbering creatures were happy. When the thin wolves moved on, the people and bears and rabbits grew angry and awoke and fought with each other. Pouk watched the wolves do this over and over throughout the long night, then they loped to the mountains as the sun rose. Pouk watched where they went and saw the entrance to the cave, which before then had appeared to be a sliver of shadow on the rock face at the bottom of a dark canyon deep in the mountains.

"Pouk waited until the last of the anger-diseased wolves slinked into the cave that early morning, then blew hot breath on the entrance, preventing the angry wolves from ever leaving the cave again. Pouk did not know that other creatures could still enter the cave, and when they finally left it again, they were changed. This, Pouk failed to notice.

"And so it came to be that the Alooknok were born, for legend tells that over time, the cave was discovered by people, even though they had been warned by elders never to venture into the dark places of the mountains. But there are always people who need to know why they have been forbidden to do something, so badly that they do not heed the warnings. They go forth and they discover much, though sometimes bad things. And so it was with the cave of the angry wolves.

"Those people were forever marked by unhappiness and rage and anger and evil and lived alone in the mountains, in the shadows. People from the tribes would sometimes see them, and recognize them for what they were—phantoms, spooks, evil spirits that dwelt in the portal of the other world, the world of evil and anger. It was said that sometimes people lost in the mountains would be found and eaten by the cave dwellers, people who eat people. Except they were no longer people, were they?"

Despite my hard effort to keep my eyes open, I had once again closed them and listened to Winter Woman tell me the story. I opened them to see her regarding me.

"It's an interesting story. Fanciful," I said.

She shrugged and stood, raising her arms and stretching her neck. "It is not for you to believe or disbelieve. It is so because the legends say it is so."

That thought sounded to me a whole lot like the claims the zealot thumpers make. No wiggle room in their thinking. But then she smiled once more. Heck, I thought she might even laugh. "Do not worry," she said. "I do not expect you to believe it. But you have to admit it sounded pretty good."

"You mean you made it all up?"

Again, she shrugged. "Some of it. I spend a lot of time with Maple Jack. He says I tell windies nearly as good as he does." She leaned close. "I think mine are more fun. His are sometimes silly and go on too long, especially if he has been at his jug."

I chuckled. "Can't argue with you on that score. Though I will admit, he is pretty good at stretching the truth and making his version of events fit most any situation."

We sat in silence for a few moments. "Do you think you can help them to get well?" I asked.

She paused for a long moment, then looked at me. "No. They cannot become well here, living underground like this. They will never learn when springtime has come." She shook her head. "They will die here, because they do not want the help they need. They want the help they think they need."

That's when Knife Thief shambled in, moving quicker than usual. He had that look on his face again. The one that said, "I'm angry at the world because I'm sick and I live in a cave." And then, as he had done several times since I made his acquaintance, he surprised me.

He stood before me a moment, looking me up and down as if sizing me up. Then he squatted and laid his spear beside him, and beckoned me to do the same. I don't normally squat, but I hunker okay. So that's what I did. I also did my best to ignore the stink drifting off the man.

Winter Woman sat still, watching but saying nothing.

Two feet from him, I noticed how very thin he was beneath his ratty draping of paltry pelts. He looked as though I could prod him with a finger and he'd collapse like a pile of desert-bleached mesquite branches. He'd make a hollow, clunking sound as his bones rattled to the floor.

I was tempted, but some part of the story Winter Woman told me stayed my hand. Here was a thin wretch whose people were dying and he could do nothing about it. My sliver of pity didn't keep me from wondering where in the few folds of his clothes he'd hidden my knife. I thought my question had been answered when he reached beneath a particularly rank-looking pelt, squirrel, I think. I tensed.

He pulled out something wrapped in cloth, filthy cloth, but cloth, nonetheless. He held it in both hands. Whatever it was, I saw beneath the cloth that it had squared edges. And I fancy I saw those blackened claws shaking, as if what he held was sacred or precious and he was afraid of it somehow. He looked at it with wide eyes and then he swallowed. His eyes shifted up to my face and he nodded toward the object.

CHAPTER THIRTY-ONE

I reached for it, keeping an eye on the rascal in case he flinched or got that smiley look again. Who knew what sort of trap he was setting for me? He and his clan were mighty primitive, but they had also gotten the best of me a couple of times. Besides, being tuckered out from hunger and a general soreness I blamed on the snowslide, I was in no position to nudge my current fortune, good or ill, too far.

I saw no alteration on his face, so I pinched the grimy, gray cloth with two fingers and lifted a corner, then peeled it back gingerly.

Beneath the wrapping was an old Holy Bible with a brown leather cover, ragged at the edges. The bottom corner at the spine had been gnawed by some confused critter and the frayed threads of the sewn binding hung like the innards of a savaged animal. I hate to see books in bad condition, but his reverence for the old tome impressed me.

He seemed to want me to peruse it, so I did, lifting the cover gently and not too high, lest it crack or fall apart. I did not want to be blamed for further damaging the relic. The light was dim in the cave, but the smoky fire to my right lent enough glow that I could make out writing on the yellowed page facing the cover. I gently pushed on the book, which he held. He understood what I meant, and he angled it toward the light.

I read on an inside page a long list of faded names in a perfect, scrolling hand, along with dates corresponding to each name. I said the first aloud. "Jonah Bartholomew, 1682 to 1721."

I looked at him for a response, but he was too busy staring at the page, then at me, with what I can only describe as awe. It was odd. I skipped a few, then read another name. "Mary Tisdale, 1710 to 1776." More of the same reaction from him as I continued. I noticed, barring the first two, the rest of the two dozen or so names on the page were all those of women. Many of the names were illegible, or written in too light a hand for the dim conditions. Toward the bottom of the list, I read a name, the last on the page, unless it continued on the next, that brought from him his biggest response. He groaned and tears formed in his red and yellow eyes.

"Mother Ruthanne MacTavish, 1803 to . . ." There was no end date. Was she still alive? I worked the date quickly in my mind and yes, she could still be alive. She'd be an old woman by now, but it was possible.

"Is she here?" I said.

He seemed not to hear me.

"No," said Winter Woman from behind me. "That is the one they call Mama Rutha."

At mention of that name, Knife Thief gasped and nodded, snuffling. He dragged the back of a hand across his face, smearing snot and tears and dirt over his nose and cheeks.

"The sickness," I said.

"Yes," said Winter Woman. "It will be their end, I fear."

"Can you be so certain?"

"Yes."

I was quiet a moment, then I said, "And what about us?"

She waited again, so I looked over my shoulder at her. She shrugged. "I cannot tell."

I looked again at Knife Thief. He still stared at the book, at the page with the woman's name. What would he look like scrubbed clean and trimmed? Perhaps if soap and water got to him, he would melt away.

From his reaction on hearing the woman's name, I wondered if she had been his mother, or perhaps his wife. I realized then I had little idea of how old he was. He could be twenty or he could be eighty. Prudence told me it was not the thing to ask at that moment.

All this verified what Winter Woman had told me. Knife Thief and his tribe were descended from wayward travelers. What a sad fate they'd made for themselves. Did none of them try to escape? Perhaps they had, and met with an even worse doom. Or were hunted down by their own kind. Neither possibility sounded anything but grim.

The clot of anger in my throat I'd felt toward him and his tribe dissolved and left me tasting bile and pity. Within the time it takes for a person to grow old, they'd aged and changed and lost everything that made them human.

Well, I thought, closing the book's cover. *Nearly everything*. They still had the book, and more importantly, they still had their memories. At least a few of them. What they gained in return was a reversion of their selves to an inhuman, animal existence.

I wondered much then, with the longest, most haunting question of all: Was this the only way the Old World and the New World could ever meet and combine? An unwanted, shunned group of religious zealots trapped unwillingly in a location even the natives kept their distance from. I thought too much on it then, as I have since. It's something I tend to do to a fault, as Jack says. "You think too much, boy. Give it a rest and sample the jug."

I'd gladly sample a jug, but there was precious little of anything in the way of wetness available in the cave, at least that

I saw, save for the foul liquid Winter Woman had given me earlier.

"You know how they get that foul water of theirs?" I said, glancing at her.

She nodded. "There is a spring in a nearby chamber. At the back. The water is not good."

"Could it be the cause of their sickness?"

"It is possible."

"That's our only option for a drink, then?" I said, trying not to think about cool, clear water and doing a poor job of it.

"We have no choice. We must use their spring."

"I believe I'll hold out a while longer."

Something nudged me and I turned back to Knife Thief. He had poked me with one of those filthy claws of his. When he saw he had my attention, he nodded at the book still in his hands and held it toward me. Did he wish to give it to me? No, it was obviously far too precious for that. Then what?

"He wants you to read to him."

"Oh." I felt a fool then. Of course, that's what he'd want. He saw me with my copy of *Walden*, which is why he showed me his tribe's Bible. Now he wanted me to read to him. Simple. Sometimes I can be thick. "What if I refuse?" I said to Winter Woman while looking at him.

She chuckled, a short, bitter sound. "Then you will die sooner than you could."

"What does that mean?"

"He found a reason to keep you alive. You will be useful to them, to read the white man's holy words."

"But I could make up anything, how would they know?"

She tapped her temple once more. "Most of them do not speak much of their language any longer, but that does not mean they do not understand it."

I looked Knife Thief in the eyes. He smiled. Right then, I

knew he wasn't letting on all that much to me, but I bet he understood near enough of everything I'd been saying. Near enough. "If I read to you, will you let her go free?"

The smile left his face like a dropped stone. He closed the book, folded the cloth gently over it, then tucked it once more beneath his furs. I don't think grabbing him would have solved anything. He'd not take us to the cave's entrance. He'd as soon die, choked out by my hands.

Much more of this and I'd be willing to find out.

CHAPTER THIRTY-TWO

Winter Woman spoke up. "I will help you. I waited for you to ask me for help instead of forcing me to help. Still, I will do what I can. But I cannot stay here with you. This is not my place. My place is out there," she waved a hand toward the cave's entrance. "With the world."

If he understood, his face did not show it.

She kept talking. "There are others, many others, who need me and I need to help them. Living in a hole in the ground is no way to live. If you force me to do this, I will say no. If you force me to do this, I will die. And then who will help you? Huh?"

It was powerful talk. For a long moment no one said a thing. Then Knife Thief dragged his toes back and forth in front of him in a half circle, as if he were a schoolboy who'd been caught filching the teacher's chalk. He looked up and I saw the same grin on his face that he showed me when he held my knife and I didn't.

He shook his head. "Nah, nah, nah." He said it in a low, growly voice unused to speaking, then pointed his spear at me. "Kill Notabear."

So that was his plan. Blackmail. Dumb like a fox, this one.

"What does he mean?" Winter Woman said to me.

"He means," I said, eyeing the tribesman, "if you don't do what they say, they'll kill me."

"Why would they do that? It makes no sense."

"To them it does."

"I will not let them."

I leaned close so we could not be overheard. "Why not play along? At least until I can figure out a way to get us out of here. All we need to do is make it back to the entrance. Then we're free."

"There are too many of them."

"Yes, but there's one of me." I smiled to offer boldness I did not feel.

She saw through it to my doubt beneath. "You sound like Maple Jack."

"Now that's a compliment I can take all day."

"Maybe it was not a compliment." Her arched eyebrow told me she knew bluster when she heard it.

Knife Thief grunted and rapped his spear's butt on the rock floor. Three of his fellows advanced from shadow. I hadn't seen them there, and it made me wonder if they'd heard much of our conversation. None of them seemed capable of comprehending much of anything, save for grunted orders.

"Do what he says," I said to Winter Woman. "We'll be okay. I have a plan." I winked at her, still smiling. I had no plan and I bet she knew it, too.

To her credit, she nodded once to me. "I hope so. Jack tells me of his plans . . ." She looked away for a moment, but I saw a smile tugging at her mouth corners. "That's when I know I am in trouble."

I couldn't argue there. Jack is one for slapping his old horned hands together and then hopping to his feet, espousing what he calls a "grand idea!" And, as Winter Woman said, that's when we get into trouble. His grand ideas usually mean hijinks that involve life-threatening danger and, I admit, a howlingly good time in retrospect.

I can imagine what Jack was like as a young man. These

episodes also tell me there's probably more truth than yarn to Jack's stories. And if you knew half of Jack's stories, you'd find that frightening.

This line of thought got me cogitatin', as Jack would call it, on what he might do to tilt the situation in our favor. As we were in a pretty grim spot, I figured anything I did, save for getting myself or Winter Woman hurt, or worse, would be of use.

Knife Thief shuffled toward us, his spear held waist high, and pointed at me. "Notabear . . ." His mouth moved without sound as if he were chewing words, trying to figure out how to say them. "Die."

"No," said Winter Woman, stepping in front of me with her hands out.

He stopped his slow, awkward advance.

"Ma'am, don't do that," I whispered.

"Quiet." To Knife Thief she said, "I will stay. You will lead him back to the world."

Knife Thief squinted at her, then up at me, and shook his head. "Notabear . . ." He pumped his spear arm up and down, a grimy, clawed finger pointing downward.

"I take that to mean you enjoy my company and wish me to stay," I said. If he understood, he didn't let on.

CHAPTER THIRTY-THREE

Not long after that little exchange, I heard a righteous hooting and hollering and howling, like a pack of coyotes and a flock of raspy-throated ravens all balled up. I looked to Winter Woman, but she shrugged.

After our cozy repartee with Knife Thief, we had been left alone once more, so I edged to the chamber door and peered into the passage's gloom. It was so dark in there, I couldn't see but four or five feet. The racket drew closer, then fizzled far off, then drew closer again. It kept up like that, poked through with howls. It was an eerie sound—I admit the hairs on my back and arms and head prickled and goose-fleshed.

I tell you, if it weren't for Winter Woman, I would have left that chamber and taken my chances in trying to find a way out, back to the crisp air of the mountainside. But I needed her with me and she wasn't budging. I admired her dedication, but I must be more selfish than I thought I was, because I didn't feel all that much in the way of sympathy toward our captors. Even after hearing their pathetic tale.

I angled my head first to one side, then the other. My hearing in my left ear could be better. Must be because that's the side closest to the rifle or shotgun when the hammer falls.

I was about to turn back to Winter Woman when I heard a sound in the passage that was anything but the gibberish those creatures were howling out. I swore it was drawing closer. I held still and listened. Yep, it most definitely was inching closer. I

179

noted it wasn't more of the moaning, howly sounds the beast-folk had been making. No, this sound was recognizable. It was English. Or something close to it. A man's voice. A man who was either frightened out of his good wits or angry. Or both.

"Jack?" I said.

It was loud enough that Winter Woman had already bustled to my side. We exchanged looks, then peered out into the dark passage. All the while, the shouting kept on, louder and closer.

Then, with no warning, a clot of the rank, scrawny cave dwellers lurched into view not a dozen feet up the corridor, and closing fast. In their midst, lashing out like a blind dervish, I made out the frazzle-haired, wild-bearded face of my friend, Maple Jack.

His arms must have been held, pinned down by their claws, but when he freed one, it flew up with mighty force, slashing the air before them, all around them, as if the air offended him. His wild attack knocked a couple of the cave dwellers to one side, then the other. They staggered and reeled from the onslaught like Saturday-night drunkards.

Within a couple of paces, they regained their dragging hold on him. He kept on freeing himself, windmilling those buckskin-covered arms, fringe twirling in the air along with his garbled shouts that were part blue words, part made-up speech, and all Maple Jack.

They reached the chamber door as I bulled forward to grab him and help him. The cave dwellers shoved him from behind and sent him sprawling to the floor. He tumbled and somehow bowled right past me. Before I knew it, they had swarmed him once more.

He sputtered and howled like an oversize rooster and shoved them away as he regained his footing. He jerked upward and rammed one of the stringy cave dwellers on the bottom of its jaw with his bandaged head. The dweller flopped onto its back, then scrambled away. Then Jack was attacked once more. This time by a friendly face.

Winter Woman had shoved through the knot of haggard cave dwellers, setting a couple of them reeling aside, and muckled onto the still howling mountain man. "My flower! My sweet flower Jack!"

"Woman!" he shouted. "You're alive?" He pushed back from her, seized her shoulders, and stared at her up close in the dim, smoky light of the cavern. "You bad off? Did these savages hurt you?" She shook her head and, though I was some distance from them, I saw she was smiling.

"Flower, huh?" I said, moving toward them. I was nearly to them when I whacked my head on the rock ceiling. Again. I can be a slow learner.

"Roamer! You made it, too!"

I wanted to hug him like she had done, wanted to scoop him up and crush him in a bear grip, but I settled for a hand on his shoulder. I squeezed and said, "Jack! Good to see you could make it to this little party. We were about to pour the wine."

"Huh?"

"Kidding," I said. "I am amazed you made it this far with your banged-up head and foot."

"Nothing amazing about it, boy. It takes a whole lot more than a few demons to keep Maple Jack from tracking his pard and his best girl."

"Oh, my sweet candy Jack," said Winter Woman. "I am so happy you are not dead."

"Me, too, woman!" Then he jerked his head back as if he'd been slapped across the chops. "Wait a minute! You speak full-bore English? Why didn't you ever say so?"

She shrugged. "You never ask."

"Women," he said, looking at me with his eyebrows high and wide.

She smacked him hard on the backside and giggled.

I did my best to not watch. It was a side of Jack I'd not seen much of. I didn't need to see any more of it.

The dwellers, led by Knife Thief, closed in once more, this time on all three of us. To a person, they were seething, with a hot look in their bloody eyes. I angled myself in front of my friends, tired of the foolishness and ready for it to be over with, sickness or no. Winter Woman would have to figure out a different way of helping them. My part was half done. I'd found Maple Jack and Winter Woman, both alive and, for the most part, healthy. Time to go.

Then she ruined my brand-new plans by edging between me and Knife Thief once more. "Leave us!" She pointed toward the door beyond a dozen of them, still panting and reeling from escorting Jack in.

Knife Thief growled but did not budge. He poked that spear past her toward Jack. "Men men!"

It was a word from him I'd not heard before.

"What does that mean?" I said to him, but he kept staring at Jack and said it again.

"Means I ain't alone!" said Jack. "Don't mean I know them others, nor do I like them, neither."

"What others?" I said, but Winter Woman interrupted me once more by shoving her arm against my midsection, as if to stifle me. "Go!" she shouted to the dwellers. "Leave now. Go or I will not help you!"

That finally seemed to get to them. They drizzled back out through the chamber's entrance, all but Knife Thief, who stood inside the doorway, glowering and growling. He was very good at it. I almost told him so, but I figured it might not go over well.

I half turned to look at Jack, then glanced back, but Knife

Thief was gone. "Jack," I said. "Glad to see you're alive. You have any weapons on you?"

CHAPTER THIRTY-FOUR

"Same with you, you big brute! But naw, naw, those men I come up here with, wolfers they were, they stole everything from me but my topknot! Wait'll I get my hands on them." He patted himself down and then smiled and tugged out a folded paper and kept it that way, though he wagged it at me. "Me, too, boy. Me, too."

I realized then it was the note I'd left him. That meant any hard feelings I'd imagined he'd felt toward me were but that, imagined. That was a mighty relief.

He stuffed the note back into some mysterious place in his buckskin tunic and turned away, sniffing a bit.

I, too, had to clear my throat. After a moment, I said, "What wolfers, Jack?"

I had to ask it over and around Winter Woman, who was busy pinching and kneading his bearded cheeks like dough. He didn't seem to mind. It came to me that there was a whole lot more to Maple Jack than I knew. And I've known him for a good many years. Still a mystery, he is.

She escorted him over to the stone seat and made him sit down, then knelt in front of him and held his bum foot in her lap and began gently unwrapping it. I don't think he'd touched the bandages since I saw him. I felt a small glow of pride noting they, and the swaddling on his head, had held up during what must have been one hell of a journey up here.

In true Maple Jack fashion, he began his explanation so far

back, I shifted my feet to get comfortable. Jack is not a man to be rushed, especially when a story is in the offing. He proceeded to tell us all about his trip.

"I come to in the cabin. It was awful dark and cold, it was. I believe it was the sound of my bones rattling and clunking together that drew me off my death bed. I gained my feet, but then I fell right over because this one here," he rapped on his right leg, "is all busted to hell. Least the ankle is. How I knew is because while I was crabbing around on the floor, I saw it was swaddled. Same as my head. That put me in mind of you, Roamer, seeing as how you're the one person I know who will wrap a wound quite like that. Must have been a draper in a past life." He winked.

"That's when it come back to me, the attack, them stealing Winter Woman away, her yelping for me. I recalled that one of them had sneaked around behind me, clubbed me on the bean, but it didn't do the job. I got worked up some, so one of them clouded my face with some awful-smelling powder, as if I were a stage actor. That's when things went south on me. Those creatures turned into demons right before my eyes! Then they attacked me and left me for dead. Next thing I know, I see your big face looking at me. I do believe you were trying to feed me tea. Tasty stuff, it was. I made more once I got the fire going. Then I fell asleep again."

I didn't dare ask anything about his experience under the spell of the rot root powder. If his memories from it were anything like mine, they were best left to linger in the dark corners of his mind. I also didn't mention the tea being more than tea. He'd get riled all over again and we'd never make it to the end of the story.

"What about Tiny Boy and Mossy?"

"What about them?"

"I left them in the stable. Were they all right?"

185

"Course they were. I made it out there. You fed them up, left the door to the corral open. Better than a greenhorn would have done. Anyway, once I got myself righted around, I dosed 'em up with feed myself, then I knocked down the gate rails. They'll make out. It was an early snow. The ground's bare enough in the low country by the lake that they can forage."

That reminded me of something I'd forgotten to ask Winter Woman. "What about the donkey?"

Jack pulled a dark look. "Oh, that cantankerous little rogue." Then he flashed her a smile. "She loaned him to a young couple expecting a bairn down the valley from her cabin. We'll see him again before long, likely lugging a little woman who's tight-to-the-hide."

In Jack-speak, I knew that meant the woman was close to birthing.

"Anyway, we'll scare up Mossy and Tiny once we get back."

"If we do," I said, wishing I hadn't.

"I never seen the like." He looked at me as if I had sprouted a second ugly head, then looked at Winter Woman. "You seen the like in all your days? Give up like that." He tried to snap his fingers but it didn't work. They're too gnarled and stiff most of the time.

I sighed and changed the subject. "So how did you make it all the way up here, anyway?"

"What do you mean?"

"Well, your ankle's still paining you, that's plain to see, and your head must still be addled because you're taking a longer time than usual to get to the point of your windy."

"Why you, whelp!" He reached out to rap me one but I ducked away, giggling. For a moment, I forgot where we were. He leaned back once more and resumed his story.

"After I finished with them, I fed myself up once more. By then I could see two of everything instead of four or five as when I awoke, so I figured I was about as good as I was going to get. I strapped on my snowshoes and tracked you, and here I am." He grinned.

"There must be more to it than that, Jack. I stuck those snowshoes up in a tree."

"Yep, you did. Don't you know by now there ain't a tree in all the Shining Mountains Maple Jack can't climb like a wildcat?" He shook his head to show his disgust with me.

I ignored him, but loved hearing his tall-tale telling. "What happened next?"

He grinned again and looked around him, as if he were about to reveal a secret. "This is where it gets interesting. See, it was oh, a week or two into my journey—"

"Jack, we've only been gone a few days."

"Oh, well, I've been addled in the head, I tell you. It's not my fault I can't recall such foolish details! Now, where was I?"

"The wolfers."

"Yes!" He smacked his hands together. "I've decided I'll keep you around, boy. Might prove useful yet." He rubbed his chin in thought. "Okay, so miles up the valley I come onto this camp, if you can call it that. Smelled it before I got there and I knowed I wasn't alone in the hills. These men, whoever they were, took no care to blend into the world about them. They were savages, I could tell from the stink of the place, even before I clapped eyes on their camp and goods. It was a mess, skins everywhere, those people can't skin a beast to save their . . . well, their hides. God-awful.

"Didn't spy nobody around, so I didn't see harm in warming up by their campfire, maybe gnawing on a hank of meat. But the longer I looked around, the more I realized nobody with good intent could possibly keep a camp like that. Reeked of meat gone off in the sun and hides poorly cured. Least a trapper or hunter can do is treat the critter he's killed with respect, honor them for taking their life by taking care with the hide.

"Not these fellas. No, sir. They barely flenched fat from hide, left withered hunks hanging off it. They showed terrible irreverence to those critters. Wolf pups even, can you imagine? I vowed then that if I made it on out of these hellish peaks, I'd stop back there on my way out and down, put a torch to the place. It's the only thing I can do for the poor beasts they slaughtered."

He hung his head and shook it side to side. "Worst treatment of beasts I have ever seen in all my days, and that's saying something because I've seen a whole lot, believe me you, mister. It being winter, it shouldn't have stunk near so much as it did, but their leavings were so bad the whole place reeked even in the cold!"

Jack shoved to his feet and paced in a circle. He ground his knuckles into the other hand's palm. "Biggest mistake I made was stopping at that camp. But I figured there might be sign of you or Winter Woman."

He shrugged, a movement I recognized from seeing her do it several times. Like an old couple. Then I realized that's what they were, and it brought a smile to my face. "What'd you do then, Jack?"

He looked at me as if I'd insulted a lady before him. "Don't rush me, boy. I'm working up to it. I've been through a trying time, you know."

As if we hadn't, but I said nothing.

The irony behind his comment must have caught up to his mouth, because he shrugged once more. "Well, bad as it was, I was hard up for warmth and I saw they had a fire going. Or at least one that was smoking. So I shouted, 'Hello the camp! Hello the camp!' loud enough anybody who wasn't stone deaf could not fail to hear.

"No sounds came back to me, and I was growing colder standing there, so I scuffed over to the fire ring, smack in the middle of their foul camp. Seeing it all up close was even worse, but seeing that fire smoking away was too much to resist. I knelt down and poked the coals with a stick, then leaned in and blew on it. I found a small, leaning pile of snapped wood close by and laid a few pieces on the young, tender flames."

Only Maple Jack could make a campfire sound so poetic, I thought.

"I had resolved to stay put and warm myself as much as I was able, then if the owners of the camp still weren't back, I'd depart and to the devil with them. It wasn't like I was stealing— who can steal fire and smoke? Not me, I tell you. Never been that clever. Not a word, Roamer!" He held up a meaty, grimy finger at me, that eye twinkle nearly visible in the near dark of the cave.

I glanced at Winter Woman, but she still sat passively, staring at Jack. Waiting for him to continue? Waiting for him to shut up? I had no idea. I couldn't read the emotions on her face.

"I was about done warming my fingers when I heard a *click-click* sound behind my right ear. Now I am normally possessed of the hearing of a wolverine. In fact, my hearing is so keen I can hear a timid finch break wind near a half mile away."

If I didn't know Jack so well, judging by the grave look on his face, I'd swear he was telling the whole, bald truth of the matter. But I knew him. Funny thing is, when Jack tells you a story, he's so involved in it that I get the impression he believes every single word he's sharing.

"You sure you didn't doze off, Jack?" I said, doing my best, and failing, to hide a smirk.

"Why you . . . ungrateful whelp! Course I didn't fall asleep. What do you think I am? Some overgrown greenhorn who falls into holes? Ha!"

I took the jab as it was meant, then wondered how he knew about my misadventure. It would come out in its own time.

He looked at his hand and shrugged. "Could be I grabbed hold of a wink or two. But I was tired, more tired than most any man has ever been in all their days. I mean . . . tired." He let his shoulders sag. "Where was I? Oh, yes, the clicking sound. Of course it was a man with a gun. I didn't move, partly because he told me not to. Mama raised only smart children." He winked and nodded.

" 'What do you want?' I said.

" 'No, no, man,' said a wheezy voice close by my ear. It was one of them, I could tell by the stink of him. 'You got it backward. You trespassing, not me.'

"Well, sir," said Jack. "I breathed deep and wished I had a wad of chaw. Always makes me think harder. Better yet, I recall wanting a pull on a jug. But that was far behind me."

"What did you do?" I said.

"What could I do? Normally, I'd spin around quick as a rattler and seize that ragged bastard's gun, snatch it from him, then knock him cold with it. But I was still ailing, so I played it quiet for the time being. 'I was only looking for some warmth,' I told him. 'Mighty cold up here in the hills this time of year.'

" 'Yeah, so why you up here if you knew that?' he asked me.

"I tried to turn to face him, I don't like talking to someone I can't see. He wanted none of it and rapped me hard enough above my ear with the barrel of his revolver that I felt hot pain and saw sprinkles of stars before my eyes, and it was still daylight. Whilst I was dazzled, he took my belt 'hawk and my possibles bag! Why, he's lucky I was already addled, elsewise I'd've let him have it. But he backed off. I reckon he could sense what sort of danger he was in. And that there's how I come to be captured by those varmints."

CHAPTER THIRTY-FIVE

"That doesn't explain how you came to lead them here," I said, not trying to make it sound like an accusation, but I guess it did, considering how Jack responded.

"You whelp, I was getting to that. No time for anything nowadays. You young folks got no patience, have you?"

He shook his head and massaged the knee above his bum foot. I felt bad about it. I normally love hearing Jack's stories, and I was beyond happy to see him whole and not permanently plagued in the head by that beating he took. But I wanted him to save his story for later once we were free of this place. "We have to figure a way to get out of here, Jack."

"Now you got me confused," said Jack. He looked at Winter Woman. "I thought you weren't leaving until she'd taken care of these cave critters?"

"I meant we need to get out and deal with those men you brought up here," I said.

Again, I saw him wince. When will I learn?

"Sorry, I don't know what else to call them."

"Try weasels and killers and thieves, for starters." He folded his arms over his chest and looked away.

I'd apologize later and smooth out things between me and Jack. Right now, we had a problem to figure out. "What say we trap them like weasels, then?"

That snared his interest. "Got a plan?"

I nodded. "Working on it."

191

"Good," he said, leaning back against the rocky wall. "Let me know when you got it figured out. I'll be over here, catching up on my sleep."

I nodded, not that he would see, and did my best to forget I'd offended my oldest and only friend. Instead, I tried to figure out how to get us out of there and lay low the vicious bastards who were, at that moment, also trying to get us out of there.

Great, so we all wanted the same thing. That was a start, I thought. Not a good one, but a start nonetheless.

"No," said Winter Woman. "I want to hear the rest of the story. It might help us to know more of those men."

"You see?" said Jack, looking at me. "Somebody here knows when not to interrupt a man when he has useful information he's about to reveal!"

I sighed and sat down and leaned back, looking toward the chamber's entrance. I saw no sign of Knife Thief or his fellow cave dwellers. I guessed we had time to fritter because I didn't have any idea of what to do.

"So there I was, trapped in the wolfers' camp, held at gunpoint. We waited a couple of hours, me and that weasel who'd found me. He wouldn't say a thing. You know how tricky it is to get information out of a man when he won't talk? Hard, I tell you. Finally, along come two other men. I smelled them, then I heard them, then I saw them. Rank is not the word for those boys."

"What is?" I said.

"What?"

"You said rank is not the word. What is the word?"

"Roamer, you give me one more smidgin of lip and I'm liable to forget I have a stoved-up leg and an addled pate. One more!" He held up a callused old finger and wagged it at me in a manner most menacing. At least for Maple Jack.

"Now, let's see. So, these three other fellows come along and

I thought, 'Here we go, I'm done for.' But nope, they thought I was a source of amusement or sport or something. I overheard them chuckling and telling each other what they were going to do with me. Then they commenced to drinking. I was of two minds about that. Now, most often, folks when they get themselves good and tight will become belligerent and unreasonable. I say most folks because, as you know, Roamer, that is not how I am."

Winter Woman snorted. Jack looked at her with shock. "You say something?"

She didn't reply except to smile. That flustered him. He cleared his throat and went back to his windy.

"They drank and drank and passed the bottle and didn't offer me a drop. Now that hurt, I tell you. Nearly as bad as the green hide straps they bound me with, getting tighter as they dried."

"Did they say what they were doing up there? I never saw sign of them on my way up the valley."

"Course you didn't. You took a different path than I did. I marked where you were, but I ventured off it because I smelled smoke from their fire. Figured I'd find someone friendly to break bread with, then snowshoe back up to your trail and out of there. That's not how it worked out, though.

"As to what they were doing, they had scouted the valley and hills about there in the summer, looking for a place to trap, shoot, hunt, skin out whatever they could find. Since there's plenty of game hereabouts, they were successful at the killing part. Trouble is, nobody told them not to waste an animal's life if they're not going to eat it.

"I told you, they left the carcasses in heaps and chucked snow on them. Terrible. It's going to be foul once springtime rolls in. They were really after wolves, though. Said they saw some mighty specimens in the summer up here and they figure

193

they can get top dollar for good hides. Trouble is, they can't skin a squirrel. Once they shot those wolves, they'd ruin those pelts. All such a waste.

"But while they were talking, they said how they'd been keeping an eye on a huge creature they took to be a shaggy bear still roaming the mountainside. Figured it was late to its hole-up for the winter. That was their word, 'roaming,' and right off it put me in mind of you, Roamer, because I recalled you had that great big buffalo robe coat you like to sport in the wintertime."

"Why, thank you, Jack," I said.

"Wasn't a compliment, boy." But I saw a corner of his woolly moustaches twitch. "Though I figure that means I saved your life. Again." He winked at me. I still don't know how he figured any of that could be mistaken for him saving my hide yet again. The workings of Maple Jack's mind are not something I care to prod too closely. Something might bite.

"I didn't want to point out to those idiots that a bear wasn't likely to be wandering around on two legs in the middle of an early storm up there. But it's been known to happen.

"They must have thought something similar, because they said it looked to them as if the bear was doing a lot of walking on two legs. Then they saw the bear's tracks, and that they were snowshoe tracks, so they knew what was what. They ain't what you'd call sharp knives, those boys." He tapped his head and shook it.

"That's when they decided it had to be a lone trapper horning in on their territory, so they made up their minds to kill him. Which would be you, Roamer. Anyway, they followed a bit, but then there was a snowslide and they figured it did the job for them, and carted off that thieving trapper-bear of a man. Figured they'd go back to search downslope the next day, as it was growing dark. They marked their progress and they did go back the next day. That's when they saw something that made them sound sober for a few minutes.

"Said they saw this bear climb up out of a hole in the ground, and for sure it walked on two legs. I saw then they still weren't certain it was a man and not a bear. That much stupid has got to be painful.

"But that wasn't the bit that got them all lathered. No, sir," Jack shook his head. "It was the creatures that captured the big bear. Yep, they said creatures, and they were not a little rattled. I kept my mouth shut, but I wondered if these 'creatures' were men, maybe a winter tribe, the ones you and me was on the scout for. I kept to myself on my side of the fire, but I listened to every word. As they described them, they sounded to me like the very demons from hell who made off with Winter Woman and left me for dead.

"I couldn't help myself and asked the wolfers: 'What happened to the creatures? Did they kill the shaggy bear man?'

"I had to know, Roamer. I was worried you'd tangled with those rascal demons. But I should have kept my mouth shut, for if I had they might well have passed out from too much liquor and forgotten about me. Then I could have escaped in the night. Curse me for being the curious sort. It's a lifelong plague. They looked at me and I could see in their wet eyes they were remembering I was there. Fresh sport, I was to be. Yes sir, I could see it in their eyes. That's when they came at me."

CHAPTER THIRTY-SIX

" 'Why are you up here, anyway?' said a tall wolfish-looking rig himself, with long, stringy black hair, greased not like some tribes do with intention, but from neglect. There was bugs fairly hopping and popping off his topknot. He's head of the outfit, easy to see, as the other men all seemed to cower before him like whipped pups do before a harsh master.

"Asked me why I wanted that big, hairy fella they'd been tracking. He went on and on like that, pestering me with questions on questions, never letting a body answer one before he jumped onboard with another. Downright infuriating, I tell ya. The nerve of some folks to talk, talk, talk, and never let anybody else get a word wedged into a conversation!"

I said nothing. I don't think Jack knows how amusing or infuriating he is. The man is a regular conundrum. I bit my cheek and waited for him to resume. And he did.

"Then he shut right up and stared at me. The other two did the same. Got downright creepy, them mangy varmints looking at me like I was a sizzling steak on the fire. Then the boss man, he rested his long, grimy hand on the butt of his big ol' hip knife, a bone-handle thing that looked to be well worn. His filthy fingers tapped and tapped, waiting on me to answer him. I didn't know where to begin, so I jumped right in, not being accustomed to much chatter or the making up of a truth. So I said, 'That big hairy fella is my partner,' I said. 'Or at least he was. Rascal that he is, he stole from me! Turned on me and now

I aim to track him down and kill him.'

"That shocked them a little, I can tell you. So I kept right on.

" 'Was doing fine, too, until you fellas up and stopped me. I am on a mission, a killing mission, and you three ought to know I aim to follow through with it.'

"They all looked at each other and chattered a bit and nipped off the jug. Finally, the tall one said, 'What sort of work you say you do?'

"I told him, 'I didn't say, now that you bring it up. But seeing as how you've caught me unawares, I will tell you we was prospectors. I say *was* because he savaged me. That's how I come to wear bandages on my pate. And why my foot is swelled up like a pine stump. I get ahold of him and do the deed, I'm through, I tell you.'

" 'For vengeance, then? Nothing more?' Boss man gave me a long look, like he was sizing me up. 'You ain't horning in on our territory, are you?'

" 'Nope,' I said. 'Got no urge to shoot critters and skin them out. I got me fatter fish to fry, mister.'

" 'How much fatter?'

"I could see by then they were slipping from my grasp. The two junior weasels were leaning back, like they already decided something. And that tall one, he had collected his skinny legs beneath him like he was about to spring across the fire at me.

"I did what I had to do, Roamer. Don't mind telling you."

I shrugged. "Anything you had to do to stay alive, Jack, is fine by me." Though in truth, I couldn't see where he was going with this story. "What did you do, Jack?"

He cleared his throat and didn't look at me. "I . . . I told them a windy."

"That's nothing new for you," I said, tamping down a smile.

The look of genuine surprise on his face shocked me. He couldn't really think I thought he wasn't a yarn-spinner.

"Well, it's more than that, Roamer. I . . . I told them you stole from me, as I said, but that wasn't the worst of it. I also told them you stole a map to a great hoard of Spanish gold lost for a hundred or more years in these mountains!"

"That's not so bad, Jack. I imagine there likely is lost Spanish gold all through the Shining Mountains. Doesn't mean it doesn't exist because we haven't seen it yet."

He smiled and smacked his hands together. "See! Right there, that's why I keep you around, boy. You know the perfect thing to say. Okay! Maybe we will find ourselves some of that gold one day, Roamer. Maybe we will."

From behind us, I heard a snort. It was Winter Woman silently chuckling at us. I'll wager to her such a moment might seem silly, but to me, it was another in a string of honest, memorable moments I've shared with my mentor. Then he went and spoiled it.

"Didn't matter none. I could see they thought I was full of beans. The leader said, 'Why don't we kill you off now and go take that map from him ourselves!'

" 'Well,' I said to those fellas. 'Because . . .' You can see I had not expected them to think that through in quite the way they had. They were drunk, but not stupid. On second thought, that might be giving them too much credit. But I saw I was going to be in even more trouble, and quick, so I said, 'Back when me and that big goober were still pards, we split that map in half, see. So he only has half of the map.'

" 'So where's your half?' said the tall fiend, standing up. I did my best to stand, too, but as I was bound hand and foot, all I did was sort of roll onto my side. He stood over me, weaving and looking down at me like he was about to slick free that knife of his. I tried to point to my head but my hands were tied, so I jerked it back and forth. It set my mind to buzzing and dizzying again, so I said, 'It's in my head, curse you! I burned my half. Committed the map to memory. I have a superior mind. So the more you whomp on me, the worse my brain gets, and pretty soon I'll be so addled you'll never find that Spanish gold!'

"The big weasel looked over his shoulder at his two partners, who were squinting, trying to puzzle out what it was I said. He looked down at me and I saw he was thinking hard, too. Painful, it was, to watch."

Jack leaned back and looked at me and Winter Woman. "That's when I knew I had them!

" 'What if I don't believe you?' that tall goober finally said.

"Well now.' I pretended to mull this over, scrunching my eyes and staring off into the night. Finally, I looked at him and said, 'Tell you what. You help me track down that big hairy galoot you saw and we'll split the takings. After we fetch his half of the map, that is!'

" 'How do we know he has it?'

" 'Because I know what I know and I saw what I saw. That ol' pard of mine is too dumb by half to fix that map in his memory like I did.' Once more, I nodded my head. 'I saw him fold it up and stuff it in his pocket, you dolt!' I'm afraid I got myself a bit riled at that point. 'Close to his heart, that's where it'll be when we find him, too! The man never takes off his clothes, let alone gives himself a full-bore dunking in a river like any civilized fellow ought to do! So it'll be there, you heed my words!' "

It was my turn to feign righteous rage. After all, Jack had all but called me a low-down, thieving, smelly skunk of a fellow who would leave his pard high and dry for the wolves to feast on. I like to think I'm a little kinder than that. Alas, all I did was snort, but Jack let it pass, hoping, I suspect, that I might be too infatuated with his odd story to recognize the picture he'd painted of me. Ha.

"So that commenced our journey," said Jack. "We been at it,

oh, I don't know how many days. It's been grueling."

"Jack, it's only been a few days since I left the cabin. You must be more addled than you think."

"Bah! I know what I know, you whelp! Now don't interrupt a man when he's telling you notions of great import. Where was I?"

"I believe you were in the midst of relating a notion of great import to us." I glanced at Winter Woman and she cracked that slight smile. Jack ignored us and picked up his story once more.

CHAPTER THIRTY-SEVEN

"We walked on from their camp. I tell you, I'm mighty glad I had my snowshoes, as that storm, then that snowslide, dumped a pile more snow than I expected it would for one so early in the season. Them fellows was sickly the next morning with the whiskey jitters—I've heard how folks who can't hold their liquor are inclined to such things. Not me, mind you, never been afflicted."

Now that was another of Jack's perennial fibs. Mornings after he's sampled too deeply of the jug, he totters around camp claiming he has a "touch of the morning ague." Ha again.

"I was stuck in the middle of their pathetic pack, so before we'd walked more than a few hundred feet, I growled at them and stormed by, leading the way. I had half a hope that they'd grow too tired or be too whiskey weary to keep track of me and I'd outpace them. But it didn't happen that way. The skinny one said, 'Hey, old man!'

"Imagine that, calling me an old man. Anyway, I pretended I didn't hear him and I kept on walking. Soon enough, he shouted again. Same thing, I kept on stomping along in your big ol' bull path, Roamer. That's when a bullet sizzled by my right ear. Close enough I can still feel that whisper of a furrow it bored in my cheekbone. That time, I stopped. I might be a whole lot of things, but stupid isn't one I lay claim to. Or at least not willingly."

I said nothing.

" 'You think you going to lose us, is that it?' said the skinny, foul leader of the three.

"I didn't say a thing. Figured I'd leave that to him to do. He did.

" 'Not gonna happen. What is gonna happen, if you keep on like this, I'm going to shoot you in the back, leave you for the wolves to feast on. But not before I take them snowshoes and anything else of yours I fancy.'

" 'What about the map? The gold?' I said.

" 'Shoot, old man. I have high doubts you had a map to begin with. Even higher doubts that there is such a thing as an old Spanish gold hoard stuffed in the hills somewhere hereabouts.'

" 'Tell you what,' I said. 'You cut these leather wraps on my wrists and I'll stick close. But I aim to be in the lead. I see that big bastard, I'm going to have at him first!' " Jack looked at me. "Had to play it up, you know."

I nodded.

"Well, that tall drink thought about it, and finally nodded and pulled out that big knife and cut my wrists loose. Then he wagged the tip in my sniffer and threatened me. 'You even try to think about running off, I'll know it and I'll end you when and where I see fit. You hearing me, old man?'

"I swallowed back the strong urge to bite his face off. But then I'd likely catch a rare disease by being close to such a rat. I turned and walked back to the front of the pathetic little line. From behind me, I heard the man say, 'What you going to kill that big hairy fella with, anyway? We got your gun and your tomahawk!' He brayed like he'd said something genuinely funny. I did not find it to be. I bit the very inside of my own mouth and kept on walking. He asked me again, and I learned he was not the type you ignored and hoped they'd go away. I stopped and without turning I said, 'My bare hands will do. I've done it before, I'm game to do it again, I reckon.'

"That shut him and the other two up once more.

"I knew I was on the right trail. Mostly because there was only the one trail. Them three had gotten as far as that hole, and a bit further, from what they told me. I was curious to know what-all they'd been talking about, so I kept up a solid pace, and me with my bum ankle. Yet I walked on, slow enough for those fools to keep up. But they are made of harder stuff than I thought, because they dogged me pretty good.

"Finally, we got to within sight of that hole of yours, Roamer. Only I didn't know that's what it was at the time. I'd seen a boulder from a distance. That's when the leader, he says, 'Yonder's that hole. We'll take us a rest there.'

"I nodded but didn't reply. Fine by me, I thought, as I was tired, too. When we got to it, I saw there was a pile of snow trampled and stomped around it. It was a curious thing. I edged to my right around the lower rim of the hole, as I didn't trust that those three might not have conspired behind my back to shove me in. I peered down into it.

"By that time, the sun was well in hand, not high noon but close enough that I could see what lay in that rocky hole. And it wasn't promising, mostly because there was nothing else in there save for a log with chinked-in steps. It looked to be busted and sagged and out of reach, even if you bent low and had someone hold your braces or boots to keep you from pitching in, headfirst.

"I puzzled over it some, figured you might be fool enough to fall in there. But it wasn't no natural-made hole. No sir, that was carved by man, no doubt about that. You was lucky to get up and out of there."

I nodded. He was right, of course. Being stuck down in that hole would have been slow, certain death. I can't help but shudder when I think back on my brief time in there, and swear to always keep an eye for where I set my feet.

He continued, "Those tracks, I saw, led all about the hole, and some of them were what I was dreading and hoping to see, all at once. They were barefoot. Like the demons who beaned me and took her!" He gestured toward Winter Woman.

"At that point, Roamer, I hoped you used them to get out of there, then laid them low once they led you to Winter Woman. But how do you kill a demon? I kept asking myself that while those three whining wolfers were licking their wounds and not looking like they were going to get up onto their feet once more and follow the trail. I worried about you both, I tell you. Roamer, I was certain those demons were bringing you back to their lair to roast you on a spit and feast on your great, mangy hide! That thought got me all worked up and I said, 'That gold won't find itself.'

"The skinny one said, 'You best calm yourself, old man, elsewise you'll be down in that hole and we'll go it alone.'

"I was about to remind them that they needed the information in my head, when one of them said, 'Map or no, I'm about tired of you, old man.'

"I turned slowly, and gave him the evil eye. He was a homely plug of a man, a squirrelly-er looking rig I never did see, all googly eyes and his mouth slavering at the corners. Chaw juice spattered down the front of him."

Jack let a shudder ripple through him and plowed on with his tale. "Finally, they got tired of being even more useless than they were and got to their feet. I considered shoving them in the hole whilst they stood there stretching and yawning and moaning and groaning. But that tall one, he's fast with his gun and they weren't close enough for me to shove in two at once without one of them snatching hold of me and bringing me down in with them. Now wouldn't that be a pretty picture?

"We walked on and on and the day aged, and I knew those

three men were getting itchy feet to give up and walk back to their foul camp. I did my best to keep a head of steam built up and keep far forward of them. But as the day aged, they got stronger and louder and pretty soon I looked over my shoulder and saw why. They had commenced to passing a bottle once more! Can you imagine? Drinking on the trail?"

I shared Jack's reaction to such antics. Sipping out of a jug around a campfire at night was one thing, but drinking while you were out and about in the wilds was stupid.

"Wasn't long before they were catching up with me, right on my heels, they were, starting to make such noises as, 'To heck with the gold,' and other fool things drunks say. My ankle was paining me and I'd given up pretending I was feeling fine. I was limping like a one-legged man on a poorly carved stick. Round about then is when things changed.

"The trail led us down, down, down and even though the sun was still high, the shadows closed in on us. I noticed it first, them other three were too buzzy in the head to take notice themselves. I kept on, but I swallowed back a knob of raw fear a time or two, I don't mind admitting. I also had to shuck my snowshoes. They were now more of a hindrance, as we were on rocky ground more than snowy ground.

"We got to the boulders out front of this hole and started to see bones arranged on high. I saw it was a proper burial ground. It slowly came to me that demons might not have bones left to bury when they pass on. And then I wondered if demons really do pass on? Maybe they're half demons.

"Then you know what those fools did? They set to howling and laughing, and pretty soon they're shoving the bones off the rocks and stomping them! I about pitched over in a heap. I know what the Sioux do to folks who trespass on their burial grounds, let alone what demons do when their bones are desecrated.

" 'Stop that!' I hissed at them, trying not to shout in that gloomy place. Even the air was grim. It didn't do anything but make them crazier. They poked fun at me and I didn't care a whit. Other times in my life men have done such and I let them have it, but this time I kept my yapper shut. I was too nervous.

"As it turns out, for good reason. I knew something they didn't. I knew we were in the actual, genuine valley of the dead. And what's more, there ain't no escaping from it. I cogitated some on the odds of being the first person ever in the history of time to do such. But then I remembered I couldn't turn tail and run. My friends were in there somewhere. That's where the trail led and Maple Jack always sniffs the trail to its logical end.

"Meanwhile, those fools kept on whooping and stomping bones and making like monkeys. That's when I saw a shadow move. Up ahead, above us. I kept still and watched it. Sure enough, it was a skinny wraith much like one of them that got us, woman."

Jack looked at Winter Woman and she nodded, either out of politeness or because she was truly mesmerized by Jack's story. I chose to believe it was the latter because I was, too. Maple Jack might be a whole lot of funny things, but he's a heck of a storyteller.

"I couldn't help myself. When I saw that rascal watching us from on high, I gasped like I'd stepped on a rattler whilst on a midnight run to the outhouse. The figure disappeared like smoke and all I was left looking at was a shadow on rock.

"The wolfers looked at me and I tried to sound confident. I said, 'Stop desecrating this sacred space!'

" 'Or what?' said the skinny one, holding a skull in his hand, no larger than that of a child, and a knife in the other.

" 'Or I won't share the gold with you, that's what.'

"I guess it was because they were drunk or feeling the jitters of the place, too, but they'd piped down some at that and he advanced on me. Must have been the fear that freaky place put in me, for I backed up. But I could only go so far before I bumped into a wall of pure rock. I smelled the place and it stunk like wet dog and smoke. Brimstone, I imagine that's what that smells a lot like. 'I reconsider,' I told him. 'We'll split the gold, no worries.'

"Meanwhile, he leans down at me, all green teeth and long greasy hair and breath that would stop a clock, and he holds up that big gleaming Bowie knife of his and he says he's going to gut that map right out of my head! Should have done it back at camp, he says.

"Me! Can you believe that? And me without my belt 'hawk! I dodged to the side in time to avoid those other two who were trying to close in on me. But I knew I was in trouble, because unless I found a way through that maze of rock and shadow and bones and bad smells and low light, why, they would corner me and commence to carving on me. They were that riled. I bet they figured I'd led them to some fool place with no way out and the least I could do was provide them with a little fun.

"That's when the shadows I was backing into kept on going! By gaw, I fell backward and landed on my backside in near darkness. Those three saw me disappear into shadow and I heard them growling and grousing and hissing to themselves. I knew pretty soon, within seconds, they were going to get bold and step on through, too and then they'd be on me. But that's not exactly what happened. Instead, I heard them arguing, then the boss man said, 'Aw, come on out, old man. We was only funning you.'

"He sounded all sickly sweet, so bad it was about to gag me hearing him. He kept talking like that. 'You come on out and we'll all find that double-crosser pard of yours and then we'll have the map and we'll all be rich together!'

"I rolled my eyes in the dark. As quiet as I could, I got to my feet and decided to take my chances in this cave, get as far back into the shadows as I could. I figured it wasn't but a matter of time before they followed me. Problem was, the deeper into that cave I walked, the loster I got. Before long, the demons set upon me."

Chapter Thirty-Eight

He shuddered and looked about him once more, not seeing me or Winter Woman.

"What happened then, Jack?" I said.

"It wasn't hardly safe in that cave, I knew it. Had to be the lair of the demons, from the dark look of that spy I saw in the shadows and the bones and the oddness of that hellish passage out front. But I had no choice. Go back out and the wolfers were sure to lay me low. Trouble was, I couldn't see a blamed thing. I had no stick to poke on ahead and I kept rapping my bean on the awful ceiling. This place can't make up its mind what it wants to be—a cave or a chamber of torture."

I couldn't disagree with Jack, they were one and the same thing, at least in this instance. He looked as tuckered out as I'd ever seen him.

"And now those demon creatures think I'm one of those wolfers!" He shuddered and looked toward the mouth of the cave. "Never."

"They are not demons." It was Winter Woman.

Jack looked at her, and when he spoke his voice had softened, the bitterness of moments before pinched off. "I know, woman. I know. I believe you." He looked at his moccasined and wool-wrapped feet. "Got any ideas, Roamer?"

I crossed the few paces to the cave entrance. "Matter of fact, I do."

He looked up, smiling. "I figured so." He shoved to his feet and smacked his hands together. "Let's hear 'em."

"Speaking of they who are not demons," I said, avoiding Winter Woman's gaze. "Don't you wonder where they got to?" I walked to the door and peered out into the passage. I couldn't see far, but I saw no sign of any of the usual weak-looking guards. If they knew how easy it would be for me to bull past them, they would act a whole lot more afraid than they had been. But of them, I saw no sign.

"You saying we should vamoose?"

"Yep," I said, eyeing them both.

Winter Woman walked up beside Jack and looped an arm around his waist. "What do you mean, Sweet Jack?"

I can't be certain, because it was dim in that cave, but I swear the old buck blushed.

"What are you going to do?" said Winter Woman.

"Ma'am," I said. "We tried it your way for long enough. Turned out the waiting worked in our favor. But these . . . people," I still had a difficult time admitting that's what they were, "they had their chance to behave better than what they've become. They made their choices, now it's time we make ours. We have to go."

Winter Woman began to protest, but Jack held up a hand. "Roamer's right, my dear. This is no way to go about things. They're dying and us being holed up in here won't help a thing. You don't even have your poultices and tinctures and medicinals, for pete's sake."

Rarely have I seen such a look of mixed emotion on a person's face. Her eyes bore a look of defeat while she set her mouth in a grim line and slowly nodded her head, inching toward acceptance. Begrudging, but it was there.

Jack turned back to me. "How will we get out of here? Once we do, I'll bet you a dollar and a pull on the jug those wolfers will be out there."

"That's part of my admittedly weak plan. We have to convince these cave dwellers it's in their best interest to lead us to the entrance."

"Oh, ho ho! So that's your plan?" Jack shook his head. "Sorry, boy, but I've had better notions while I was knocked cold in a bar fight."

"I didn't say it would be easy."

"And if they don't? Then we're right back where we are now."

"Nope," I said. "Then we force them to."

"No killing," said Winter Woman.

"I won't kill any of them," I said, holding up my hand as if I were making a solemn oath. I wouldn't kill them, but I sure as hell would do what I wanted to do since I met them. I'd thrash and throttle and drag and do whatever I had to do to convince them we meant business. Jack gave me the narrow-eye look and nodded. He knew what I meant. Then his expression changed.

"Wait a minute . . . you smell that?" said Jack.

"Geez, Jack. Leave it to you . . ."

"No, man," he said. "I'm serious. Smoke."

CHAPTER THIRTY-NINE

"This whole place is full of smoke."

"No, not that greasy tallow stink. Woodsmoke, I think."

I sniffed. He was right. It was faint, but it was coming from the tunnel we aimed to take, somewhere in the darkness.

Winter Woman took Jack's hand and he said to me, "Lead the way."

"Okay, let's go." I stepped into the corridor. "Jack, grab hold of the back of my coat. Winter Woman, you grab Jack's. And don't anybody let go. If you do, shout so we don't lose one another. No telling where we'll end up if we get turned around in here."

"More lost, you mean," said Jack. "Now get moving, you big brute!"

Within twenty feet, it was blacker than a gravedigger's back pocket. I groped the damp, craggy walls. We crept on. I probed with my feet, tapping my way forward, and kept myself hunched low so I wouldn't hit my poor head any more than I had.

After a minute, I said, "Jack?"

He was right behind me. "Yeah?"

We kept our voices to a harsh whisper.

"You sure you don't remember which way you came from?"

"Naw. I was busy keeping those brutes—sorry, dear—those poor people from tearing the flesh off my bones. Never seen the like!"

He was getting worked up again, and with it his voice rose. I had no patience for niceties. "Shush!" I hissed. It did the trick. "Okay, okay . . ."

That's when, as somebody somewhere is once reputed to have said, all hell broke loose. Starting with the screams.

The sounds stopped us a moment. They were coming from ahead of us. I moved faster, making certain I still felt the tug of Jack's hand on my coat.

I thunked my head twice, managing to stifle a groan the first time. The second, I bit off a harsh word and muttered, "Sorry," as I rubbed my forehead. I wasn't a beauty contest winner before I got suckered into that place, and I damn sure would rank at the bottom of the list once we got out. And I vowed I would get us out. Somehow. It's easy to be confident when you can't see the things in the shadows.

The screams, as before, were random, poking through the dark like knife cuts, and made us all seize in our tracks each time we heard them. Then we hurried all the more. As bad as it sounds, the screams were helpful, as was the smoke, which had thickened, in letting me know we were moving toward the pitiful sounds. Whether they were emanating from the front of the cave or not, I didn't know. But anywhere was better than sitting on my hands doing nothing in that dismal cavern.

"What do you suppose is going on up there?" said Jack. I didn't reply right away, as I was concentrating on groping the wall with my right hand, rubbing my aching head with my left, and tapping the floor with my boot so we wouldn't tumble into a hole in the earth. I'd already done that recently and, while it was interesting, it was not an experience I needed to repeat.

I heard one, two loud cracking sounds, as if the very mountain above us was splitting apart. I winced and felt Jack's hand jerk back on my coat. Fear will tighten a man's grip on about anything. I crouched lower. Another cracking, snapping sound, and I knew it for what it was. "Somebody's shooting," I said. This was followed by more screams from up ahead, closer than before. This time it sounded like more people, too. A commotion. "Those wolfers are shooting in the cave!"

"They made it in?" said Winter Woman.

"Or they're outside, plugging away at whatever's moving inside."

We kept on walking forward, lower and slower now, fearing a ricochet bullet might seek us out any second. Under my hand, the rocky wall veered hard to the right. The smoke thickened and I heard Jack stifle a cough.

Not so with Winter Woman. She launched into a full-bore cough. Not that it would matter, as the voices, some moaning, the rest working up hacking, wet sounds, punctuated the echoes of gunfire with gasping and retching.

I led us at a faster clip, aware now that I could see shapes in the darkness and thickening smoke. That increase, however slight, plus the louder coughing and infrequent cracks and spangs of gunfire and bullets pinging off rock, emboldened me.

Before us the dim shapes took on more distinct features, features that moved. We kept low, as the smoke seemed slighter down by the floor. I abandoned the awkward notion of cat-footing and dropped to my hands and knees. Jack let go of my coat, but there was little chance of us getting separated at this point. We knew we were near the entrance.

What I saw next made me groan. The entrance, not forty feet ahead, was half filled with crackling wood, crudely stacked with what looked to be branches, flames licking and dancing, smoke rolling upward, filling the low, vaulted ceiling. Were I to stand, I could likely reach the center at its height with an extended hand.

But I wasn't about to stand.

The cave people huddled not far from us. Near the fire at the entrance, others darted back and forth, screaming—which accounted for the awful sounds we'd heard—in front of the gaping, smoking hole. They loped from side to side, past the narrow entry, behind the flames, as if taunting the wolfers.

Beside me, Jack growled. "Those foolish cave demons! Why don't they go deeper in? Don't they know guns are meant for killing?"

"I don't think they have much notion of what guns do at all." They were unafraid because they had so little experience with outsiders. We might have been the only ones since they moved in here, however long ago, to pay them an extended visit. I, for one, was ready to go home.

Winter Woman gasped and I saw her lean low over a prone body. It looked to be a frail shape, all bone, skin, and hair. I saw its shallow breaths and guessed it was one of the cave dwellers the wolfers had shot.

Between coughing fits and my tearing eyes, I saw others strewn about the floor of the rocky grotto. One or two moved. The others, perhaps four, maybe five in all, lay still.

Before I could stop him, Jack was up, walking toward the entrance, his hands held high. "Don't shoot, you rascals! It's me. Got good news—but if you kill me, you'll never know where the gold is hid!"

That stopped the hooting and hoorah-ing from the savage wolfers. One of them called out, "We're listening, old man!"

Jack was but six feet or so before me. He'd slowed his walking pace. At the "old man" crack, I heard him growl deep in his throat. A fellow can only insult Maple Jack so many times before he feels the mountain man's wrath. If he could, I knew Jack would let the wolfer have it. I aimed to make certain nothing interfered with him getting that chance. But first I had to stop him from getting himself killed.

"Jack, get back here. Let me go!" I had no plan beyond that, but I hated seeing that limping man offer himself to the wolves.

He heard me, I knew it, but he didn't let on. He kept walking. Knot-headed as a pine stump. Then he said, "Figure it out, Roamer! Back my play."

What the specifics of his play were, I wasn't certain, but his plan had to be something impressive—and straightforward, knowing Jack. I guessed it would involve me barreling in when the rogues least expected to see a bear of a man barreling. That was his favorite part. Mine, too, provided the guns were not aimed in my direction.

I looked at Winter Woman, but she was too busy tending the gasping figure. I dragged my hand across my eyes and buried my mouth and nose in my collar once more, squinting and crawling forward toward the entrance, Jack a couple of strides before me.

How he could take the smoke even a foot higher than my own head, I didn't know. But he kept on, and to his credit, the wolfers seemed to have bitten at his hook.

I was about to veer to my left, toward the shadows, when I spied something long and thin alongside the prone body of the cave dweller to whom Winter Woman was ministering. It was one of their infernal spears. Better than a spoon, I decided, and snatched it up. Then I angled to my left, where it was darker, in an effort to keep the wolfers from seeing me through the flames.

"I'm about as close as I can get to this fire of yours!" Jack shouted. "You going to rake it back out of here or what?"

There was a pause, then one of the attackers said, "Naw, you tell us what we need to know and then we let you go."

"That ain't how this is going to work, you insufferable fool!"

"Jack," I whispered, then coughed. "That's not going to help."

"I know it, got to keep them going until you get set, Roamer. You about ready?"

Even with a couple of lungfuls of smoke, I managed a sigh.

"We're waiting, you cranky old man!"

Uh-oh, that did it. Jack was on the move. "I'm coming, you brutes!"

I got my feet under me once more and, keeping as low as I was able, which isn't an impressive amount, I barreled forward. Jack stepped aside and I tore between him and the fire. As I rushed through the entrance, I kicked at the solid flaming, smoking blaze that blocked the five-foot-wide portal and sent the meat of it whipping outward.

I kept low, tucked and stomping, the spear held before me like a sword. I swung it back and forth, hoping I wasn't going to whack Jack with it.

I saw that the scattered branches and sticks of the fire were not anything a tree ever grew, save for one in the netherworld. These were bones, human bones. Before I could correct my aim, my big boots sent a couple of skulls caroming off close-by standing stones. I followed, it being fairly dark, and slammed into the big stones myself.

As I said, it was dark. The only flaw in my plan was that there was no plan. Never mind that it was Jack's non-plan. In my daze—did I mention I thunked my head into another blasted rock?—I heard barks of surprise. Someone shouted, "It's a bear! Oh god, it's a bear! We scared a big grizz out of its den!"

Another voice said, "Told you it was a bear and not no man!"

About the time I realized they had mistaken me for the bear, I heard another voice, familiar, close by my right side. "Get up, boy! Got ourselves a fight!"

I didn't need reminding. Through my stinging, tearing eyes, I made out Jack's shape beside me, then two others ahead of me. I went for them, offering up my best full-throated, smoke-addled bear growl. I had to close the gap between us before they regained their senses and squeezed a round into my non-bear hide.

The further one appeared to have bolted back up the trail,

hollering something about bears and devils and his sainted mama. If I got the chance, I vowed I'd help him meet up with her again in the near future.

Right then, I made it to the closer one without hearing gunshots, and swung a meaty fist downward, aiming for that spot where the neck meets the shoulder. Such a blow will cripple and drop a man, more often than not, as the shoulder bone isn't the toughest thing on a frame.

This clout did the trick, and for good measure my fist raked close to the head on its way down and nearly peeled off the man's ear. If he was going to live through this, that ear would be a sorry, hanging, red, swollen lump. Good.

The wolfer let out a pitiful yelp and collapsed at my feet. I kicked him a couple of times until I was certain he was not going to move for a spell. I shifted side to side on the narrow stone trail, hoping to keep myself a tricky target in the dim light. In a no-holds-barred fight, every little bit helps.

While I danced in the stony passage, I kicked at the man again. Then I bent low and groped at him in the low light, wincing because I'd not done my already-busted finger any good on its short road to healing. I found his arms. I trailed up one, nothing. Then the other, and found a revolver, still in his grip. Now in mine.

I dithered but a moment, wondering if I should dog it up the trail and track the one who escaped, but then I heard Jack ripping out a string of blue words. I spun around, the mountain's rocky face to my back, and focused on who was where.

The fire I'd kicked gave paltry light, now scattered and little more than embers and glowing lengths winking low. But it was enough to see the two hunched, warring shapes further down the thin trail, well beyond the cave's entrance. For the moment, I shoved away the thought that the smoke I'd been breathing had been the burning bones, and who knew what else, of people.

I saw one of the struggling shapes go down and that hastened my already-running frame to move quicker. I reached the wolfer in three strides as he was turning toward me. I snatched at him across his chest and spun him around, intending to deliver a piling drive to his face.

CHAPTER FORTY

"Hey, boy! Hey!"

My descending fist, which gripped the pistol, was already swinging downward in its hard arc when I realized it was Jack and not the wolfer I was about to drop.

For some reason I assumed it had been Jack who'd fallen, but, as he so often does, the crusty old mountain man surprised me. Between my shoving him away with one hand and him jerking his head back, we managed to avoid a serious drubbing.

"That's the thanks I get for saving your hide?" he cackled. But I could tell he was in high spirits.

"You do for him?" said Jack as we both leaned back against the rock wall for a quick breather.

I glanced uptrail toward where I left the man I'd clubbed. "I hope so. If not forever, at least for a nap, with a headache at the end."

"Good. And the other?"

"He hightailed it uptrail."

Jack grunted disappointment. I felt the same. It bothered me that the man was potentially still on the prowl.

"How about this one?" I said.

"This thing?" Jack delivered a kick to the man's shoulder. But it was with his limpy foot and he bit back a growl of pain. "Bastard's out cold and he's still vexing me."

"I'll find something to tie him up."

From within the cave, not a dozen feet away, we heard wailing and weird, moaning sounds.

"Winter Woman," muttered Jack, and limped for the entrance.

I bent over the prone man to strip off his belt or coat or shirt, anything to lash him tight with. That's when I felt a hot pain on my arm. He was only catnapping.

He'd sliced at me with a knife. I shoved backward, away from his reach, or so I hoped, and kicked at him. But he was wiry and wily. He spat several times, wet sounds, perhaps blood. I don't think Jack had stabbed the man, but I didn't know for certain. Didn't really matter, as the brute was up and armed and coming for me.

I rolled to my right, avoiding his grunt-driven lunge. But he was fast and scrambled at me once more, plunging that knife at me over and over as if he were a machine made for that one task. So far, he was a faulty bit of machinery.

I shoved backward with my heels, digging into the hard ground, scattering hot bones. Then I ran out of ground and clunked against the rock wall. That's when I remembered what I was holding.

A revolver isn't the most elegant of weapons. It will do the job it was built for, but it's loud and crass and smells bad and . . . nah, in a pinch like that, what's to complain about? It did the job. And it's quick. Would have been quicker had I recalled sooner I was holding the thing. By the time I did, he was crowding me again, leaning in and slashing downward with an arm that ended in a sharp steel point, a point that I did not want inside me.

My thumb yanked back on the hammer and I sent out a tiny prayer that the bear-fearing dolt I'd dropped had sense enough to load his gun before so kindly handing it over to me. He had.

The dismal scene bloomed bright with orange light and a thunderous echo. Even then, the bullet had already done what it was birthed for. It bored a hole in the tall wolfer's breast. He whipped backward and around, yet remained standing above me, weaving, eyes wide. Then he popped a couple of big blood bubbles out of his mouth and felled himself forward like an axed tree, right down on me.

It has been argued, mostly by Maple Jack, that I'm not as quick as he is. Though then again, as he claims he can best a riled mountain cat at most any contest, I assume nobody's his better in the delicate art of speedy reflexes. But I did a pretty good job of rolling to my right, out from under the toppling wolfer.

His face hit first, smacking hard against the mountain's rock wall. The man's knees buckled and his shoulder snagged for a moment on a jut of stone. I wasn't about to dislodge him. I was too busy shoving up to my knees and thumbing back the hammer on the revolver once more. I needn't have bothered. The man was dead before he toppled.

The weight of his sagging body loosened the snagged shoulder and he flopped to the ground, facedown. This time he was well and truly gone, no Lazarus acts left to him.

I looked around, making certain there were no other surprises waiting for me, and I remembered the man I'd lambasted before. I walked back up to where I'd left him, the revolver held at the ready. He lay in the same position he'd assumed when I hit him. At the time, I thought him only knocked unconscious. I knelt, alert and aware as I could be, and prodded him with my free hand, the gun aimed at his meager thinker.

Again, I needn't have worried. It appeared that somehow the blow I'd dealt him earlier had killed him.

It's one thing to lay a man low with a gun or even a knife, things I've reluctantly and not proudly had to do in the past. But rarely have I killed a man with nothing but a brute fist.

It is likely because I am large and possess more power in a swing of a fist than most men. I don't say that with any measure of pride. I say it with sorrow and shame. Killing is no way to live. It is a desperate man's last option. Or a sleazy man's easiest option.

At least that was my thinking when I pulled my hand away from the man's neck. I regarded him a moment more, then reached again for his neck to check for a blood pulse. I knew he was dead but I wished he had only been fooling me somehow. But no, he, like his boss, was dead.

"Sorry, fella," I said, and stood.

It was quick work to shove him out of the pathway. I considered dragging the other one over by him, but a shout from inside the cave nabbed my attention.

I thought briefly of the third man while I hustled back to the cave. Was he still running? Wishing, above all else, for freedom from this place of madness? I hoped so. I had no desire to mix it up with another of them.

I reached the cave's ragged entrance as someone pushed through it toward me. It was Knife Thief. He looked over his shoulder as if someone behind him might catch him at a secret task. He looked up at me and for the first time, I saw the man behind the crusted filth. He looked small and sad and old, older than I suspected. His rheumy, red-and-yellow eyes looked ready to shed tears.

Quicker than I would have credited him being, he reached beneath his ratty pelts and pulled out something. I tensed, ready to knock him on the head with the revolver.

He held out my knife, handle toward me, and nodded.

For a moment, I was tempted to let him keep it. But no, I am not as kind as that. I reasoned he had existed in his paltry way long enough without my fine knife, and I couldn't count the times in a day I rely on it. I accepted it with a nod. "Thank you," I said.

I looked down into the kindly eyes of He Who Once Was

Knife Thief. The only other time I'd seen him look that calm and innocent, childlike, had been when he showed me the tattered old Bible he'd unwrapped with such reverence. In that moment, I knew what I had to do.

I held up a finger, then reached into my own coat and offered him something of far greater value to me than the knife. I pulled Thoreau's book from my coat pocket and handed it to him.

If he was astonished earlier while staring at the Bible, he was downright awestruck holding that little hardback book in his grimy, claw-tipped hands.

I nodded once and he nodded in return. I can't be certain, as it was not the best-lit place I've ever been, but I believe he smiled. The moment warmed me a good, long while.

CHAPTER FORTY-ONE

The moaning sounds we'd heard from within the cave were its strange residents mourning their fresh dead. Three of their number had been laid low by the fiendish wolfers and their random, crazed gunshots.

"Is there anything we can do for them?" I whispered to Winter Woman.

"No," she said. "I cannot help them because the cure is out there." She nodded toward the entrance.

"Hmm," grunted Jack as he looked gloomily at the cave people.

Winter Woman shrugged and held Jack's hand. "I was wrong. I think they want to be here, on their own, to live as they choose."

"The lives their forebears chose for them, you mean," I said.

She regarded me for a long moment, thinking. Then a creature I'd not seen in the shadows beside Winter Woman shuffled forward and coughed. In a low, hoarse whisper, the shadow woman said what sounded like, "Our choice."

I was surprised to hear this little cave woman do more than growl and cough and spit. Then I recalled that Winter Woman had learned what she knew of these strange people from the women of this place.

"We were wrong to take you from your life at the feet of the mountains."

Winter Woman bent her head to the cave woman and said, "I

am not Mama Rutha and I can never be."

The little cave woman nodded. Tear tracks had traced lines down the grime of her cheeks. "We know. But we must not leave."

"Look," I said. "We could help you to live longer, better lives. Better than you will if you stay holed up here."

Jack nodded. "That's right. And don't forget about the Indians who come up here. They think you're evil spirits of the mountains. No telling what they might do one of these days."

The raggedy woman shook her head. "They are not our concern," she said. "There is a reason we must stay." She looked to her right, at Knife Thief. Those of her fellows she looked at appeared nervous. Then Knife Thief nodded, as if giving her permission to reveal some great truth. So she did.

"They will be angry."

"Who's 'they'?" I said.

Knife Thief rocked back on his heels as if he'd been smacked across the mouth. "Dwellers!" he wheezed, his voice barely more than a whisper.

"Dwellers?"

"They live in deep, dark places," said the cave woman.

I was confused. I thought that's what the cave folk were. "There are others?" I asked, wondering if the new batch was also stunted mentally and physically.

"The dwellers . . ." She gestured behind her. "Far deep in these caves, in the deep, dark places."

"Deep, dark places," the other cave people repeated, as if in a chant, in hoarse, croaky voices unused to speaking.

She must have seen the genuine confusion on our faces. The woman spoke again, her head bowed in reverence. "They live beyond us, far beyond us, in the deep, dark places. Far beyond where we live. We are their guests, their gatekeepers. They have always been here and they will always be here. We will pass but they will continue."

As she spoke her eyes rolled back in her head and she began to sway and tremble in place. The others did the same.

As if conjured, the two wan sources of light, smoking pots of lit tallow, guttered. Their flames bent forward toward the entrance before us, and a warm, dank wind pushed against us, as if urging us out, to leave this place.

Sudden voices, from somewhere far away, from somewhere deep in the past, reached us. At first, they were thin, hissing sounds. Then they grew louder, bolder, closer.

And though they formed no words that I had ever heard, they were snaky sounds that portended the vicissitudes of time itself, calamitous events to befall the earth, such things that have happened and others that have yet to be.

All of it, the past, the present, the future, all came at us in that breath from the deep. The voices mixing, swirling, screaming, shoved at us, in us, through us, forcing us to get out, out, we must get out. Before it was too late.

Some unspoken agreement between the three of us, the three not of this place, forced us to bolt for the entrance.

Jack reached it first, his old bandy legs not failing him, his knobby hand clinging tight to Winter Woman's work-hard hand. I was on their heels.

We broke out into the dim daylight, gasping and staggering. When we looked behind us, only the barest gash of blackness in the gray-black rock face indicated where the cave was. Or had been.

Of the people within, there was no sign. We three looked at each other and exchanged agreement as only people who have been through much hardship together can. Without words, we fell into line.

I took the lead and we trudged along the gravel path, through the last of the melting snow, out of the canyon of winter. The place of forever winter, knowing we would never return there. And knowing no one would ever again leave from there. At least no one in corporeal form.

CHAPTER FORTY-TWO

Five days later, after a couple of days' rest at the cabin, I stood for a moment before Jack and Winter Woman. Tiny Boy, laden with my meager gear pile, fidgeted beside me. The knife cut on my arm that the wolfer had inflicted was little more than an annoying scratch. And the broken finger on my right hand was splinted and bound tight, courtesy of Winter Woman. It throbbed worse now than it had before she'd tended it, but I didn't dare say so in her presence. When it came to doctoring, she was kindly but stern. I'd loosen it on the trail.

My traveling kit was skinnied up, missing most of what I'd lugged into the mountains, save for my knife and my Schofield (which I'll get to in a minute). As for the rest, it was a small price to pay for getting my oldest friend—and a brand-new one—out of danger.

We'd left that cave and the dwellers, or rather the gatekeepers of the dwellers, behind and didn't look back until we'd gotten the hell out of there. Well, that's not quite true. We stopped more times than I thought we might, given our fiery retreat from the cave. The first time had been not far outside the entrance, in fact. Right at the facedown, dead body of that tall, greasy wolfer.

Jack shoved him over so he lay sprawled facing upward, at what little sky was visible in that dark, rocky place of shadows and ill winds. My friend bent low and came up with his prized tomahawk and his possibles bag, which the wolfer had hung around his scrawny neck and half tucked beneath his shirt.

"Steal from Maple Jack, will you!" Jack said as he thrust each item in his waist sash and delivered one last kick to the dead man's hide. We hurried on. Several hundred yards up the rocky trail, a handful of loose pebbles drizzled down beside us.

I was in the lead and by the time I half spun and glanced upward, I saw a black shape dropping down at us. The thought of it as a lion filled my mind and I snatched for the swiped revolver. But I would have been far too late. Jack, too, was clawing for his weapon of choice, but there was no need.

From somewhere in her voluminous skirts, Winter Woman produced a gleaming dag blade that reflected the scant daylight. She thrust it skyward. I got but a momentary glance of it before it disappeared . . . into the dark shape that had dropped in near silence upon us.

It was the third wolfer. He'd been crouched on high, waiting for vengeance. But he hadn't reckoned on Winter Woman. She'd let him do most of the work, impaling himself, the full length of the blade piercing right through his vitals. Then she simply sidestepped and let him drop to the trail, carrying the gleaming steel within him all the way to the ground, all the way to his death. It was a gruesome, yet tidy piece of work on her part.

"Woman," said Jack in a cautious whisper. "You . . . you . . . didn't tell me you had a blade on you!"

Even in the low light I could see her shrug. "You didn't ask."

He said, "Huh. Women."

"Get it for me, my Sweet Jack."

"Yes, ma'am." And he did, cleaning it well on the dead man's trousers.

That incident gave us something to chew on for a spell. It also brought peace of mind, knowing we wouldn't be dogged by someone who wanted us dead. We kept our silence until, on up the trail a ways, we came upon Jack's snowshoes. Winter Woman carried those.

It continued to be a journey of discovery, soon marked by a moment of serendipity.

Normally, I don't put much stock in luck, which to me is fortunate circumstance brought about through hard work. And it's often enhanced by more hard work. That's how it has occurred in my life, anyway.

Until I see proof of something else, something more, I will keep my own thoughts on the matter. Even though Jack called me a cynic some time ago when the topic came up. I told him he should stop tossing out his two-dollar words as if they were rice at a wedding. He called me a whelp and smacked me. Or tried to.

But on this return trip to the cabin, fate or luck or serendipity, whatever you care to call it, was with us. Winter Woman said something low to Jack, who told me to hold up.

"You okay?" I said, turning.

"Yep. She's seen something downslope of us."

I tensed and reached for the strange-to-me revolver at my waist.

"No, not like that. Look." He pointed, squinting, even though the sun had for a time been gone from that east-facing flank of the mountainside. I followed his knobby finger's line of direction. There was indeed a black line visible. More than that, a curved shape, distinct but emerging from that day's rapid snowmelt. I sidestepped down the slope toward it.

It turned out to be my Schofield! As silly as it may sound, finding that battered relic of a revolver heartened me and made me realize how much I rely on it and, more to the point, how much I've been through with that gun hanging at my waist—or in my fist.

As I lifted it from the snow and wiped it off, I gave a cheerful shout up to my friends. "Hey! My Schofield!"

I vowed I'd never again grouse about having a firearm on my person. And I swore I'd do my level best to never again lose it. Of course, Jack would say, "Never say never."

Smiling, I trudged back up the slope and thanked Winter Woman for her sharp eyesight. We stood there a few minutes more, looking the spot over for anything else of mine that might have emerged. A pack, a jutting rifle barrel, a snowshoe, my mittens, my hat, anything.

We spent what time we could scouting for my scattered gear, but saw nothing else, unfortunately. Yet I felt no real annoyance, save perhaps for losing the mittens. The sentiment behind them mattered more than the mittens themselves, but their warmth would also be missed.

Not far ahead sat the rock that marked the hole in which I'd been buried alive. I glanced down once more into it. The cracked log ladder still rested in there, bent like a dog's hind leg, its far end lost to the darkness of the pit. I shuddered as I pulled back.

None of us said anything, but we resumed our walk at a steadier pace, hastened not only by the coming darkness, but by the harsh shadows below and behind us, fresh memories nipping at our heels like hydrophobic wolves.

We made good time, unhampered by snowfall, and reached the wolfers' camp as dark descended. Just as well we didn't see much of the place that night. The glimpses we got and the smells that met us as we gathered firewood and rummaged for the rest of Jack's meager supplies were enough.

We boiled water and hunted for coffee in the scant mess of goods the three wolfers had lived on. We unearthed very little, save for a handful of coarse salt, enough beans to feed a cat, and, lucky for us, a sack of cornmeal. With it, Winter Woman made a mess of tasty little cakes that she livened with dried herbs she pulled from her big apron pockets. She's a wonder.

There was no coffee, much to my regret, but Jack found an uncorked bottle of gargle that, though it smelled bad, tasted a squinch better than that, still rank but warming to our fatigued bodies.

We sat in the dismal death camp, huddled close around the fire, not wanting to venture much beyond the ring of safety we'd formed in the light and warmth, save for quick trips into the dark for our necessities. We ate, sipped the rotgut cut with warmed snowmelt, and did not chatter much. We each were lost, ruminating on our respective thoughts.

I felt the emptiness of my inner pocket where my copy of Thoreau's collection of sage, sometimes pious thoughts had nested for so many miles, for three years now. I thought of the old woman who'd given it to me, and suspected she had long since gone on, as Jack says, to take her seat of glory at the great vittles table in heaven.

I hoped that's where she was, if there was such a place. I'm still not certain. And I don't want to know for a long ol' time yet.

The old woman had told me that a book's task is to go out in the world and not stay in one place too long. I don't know how long that book will stay with them in the cave, likely forever. If there's one of them who cares to read it, if any of their number can read, I hope they take it to heart. It might well inspire them to go out into the world.

" 'I went to the woods because I wished to live deliberately . . . and not, when I came to die, discover that I had not lived. . . .' " I spoke the quote in a low voice, scarcely aware I had done so as I dwelt on the irony of its intent with the cave dwellers in mind, they who once had been human. Would they ever again know a life of their own deliberation?

"Huh?" said Jack from his spot at the fire.

"Nothing," I said. "Thinking out loud."

Jack snorted and yawned. "You and your thinkin'. I'm for sleep. It's been a day of hard wonders." He settled closer to Winter Woman and soon both were breathing deep and low.

Tired as I was, I sat for some time watching the flames pinch lower until only coals glowed. Hard wonders, indeed. Then I, too, huddled into my coat and dozed.

The next morning, early, we laid dried wood in the firepit, revived the flames, then pulled inward to the pit everything we could lay hands on that the wolfers had left behind . . . the bones, the greened skins, the poorly tanned stacks of hides, their gear and hole-filled tent, all of it.

Then we heaped more brittle, dead branches on it and coaxed the whole, sorry heap to blaze. We stood well away and watched until it collapsed in on itself. When we were assured it was no longer a threat, we walked on, a last task taken care of.

CHAPTER FORTY-THREE

And then there we were, days later, rested and healing from our various wounds suffered, some visible, some not. And parting as even closer friends than we had been. It didn't seem possible, yet it was. Strife and hardship will do that to true friends.

"If you're passing downcountry by way of my cabin, check in on it, will you?" Jack asked.

I nodded. "You bet."

"And after you get to wherever it is you think's so important you have to get to, come on back and stay a spell."

Again, I nodded, though we both knew that was not likely to happen. They needed time without anyone else around. So did I, for that matter. I needed to live on my own, and deliberately, for a while. I'd see Jack in the spring.

We'd already hugged—well, me and Winter Woman. As for me and Jack, we shook hands and cleared our throats and looked at our feet and at the pretty blue sky, and not much at the mountains looming large, never far away.

Nothing more worth saying needed saying. We all knew. I smiled and gave one last wave, then turned away, swallowing a hard knot in my throat. Every time.

Tiny Boy and I walked southeastward along the edge of the lake. I'd not given it much thought, nor do I most of the time when I choose a direction of a morning.

Not a week or so earlier, I'd been looking to spend time deep in the mountains in cold conditions. Since then, I'd had more than my fill, enough to last me a good, long while. Maybe one day I'd test my winter fortune once more in the high country. Maybe. Some other time down the trail, but not this winter.

Right then all I wanted to do was feel the sun warming my bare, sore head, take in the blue sky of this fine December day, and enjoy the quiet company of Tiny Boy, my trail mate.

Before dark we'd find a sheltered glade, build a fire, brew coffee, and tuck into that new book still waiting, its pages filled with promise, in my saddlebag.

The mountains, for now, were at my back.

ABOUT THE AUTHOR

Matthew P. Mayo is an award-winning author of novels and short stories. He and his wife, photographer Jennifer Smith-Mayo, along with their trusty pup, Miss Tess, rove the byways of North America in search of hot coffee and high adventure. For more info, drop by Matthew's website at MatthewMayo.com.

The employees of Five Star Publishing hope you have enjoyed this book.

Our Five Star novels explore little-known chapters from America's history, stories told from unique perspectives that will entertain a broad range of readers.

Other Five Star books are available at your local library, bookstore, all major book distributors, and directly from Five Star/Gale.

Connect with Five Star Publishing

Visit us on Facebook:
    https://www.facebook.com/FiveStarCengage

Email:
    FiveStar@cengage.com

For information about titles and placing orders:
    (800) 223-1244
    gale.orders@cengage.com

To share your comments, write to us:
    Five Star Publishing
    Attn: Publisher
    10 Water St., Suite 310
    Waterville, ME 04901